Like Sheep

Judy Mitchell Rich

ISBN 10: 1478336552
ISBN 13: 978-1478336556

Published by Limestone Creek Books, Athens, Alabama

This book is a work of fiction. However, members of Kipp Presbyterian Church in Kansas will recognize the setting and the "ghost" they lived with. All of that is fictionalized into the imaginary Harvest Church which is not as beautiful as Kipp. And Harvest's parishioners are not nearly as friendly. All the characters, dialogue, plot and resolution are products of the author's imagination. Any resemblance to persons living or dead is entirely coincidental, and any real settings are used fictitiously.

A picture of Jesus and the Lambs which inspired the fictional one in this novel hung in Kipp Presbyterian Church. That church closed in October of 2000 with a grand celebration of its ministries. The picture now hangs in Saint Andrews Presbyterian Church, Topeka, Kansas.

Cover Design: R. Matthew Todd

Cover photo: 1986 by JMRich

Acknowledgements

I am grateful to friends and family who read and reread this novel, giving feedback, advice, and encouragement: My sons: Matt and Mitch Todd; sisters: Susan Bryan, Sally Mitchell, Kate Murray and Becka Cartier; good friends: Valerie McLaughlin, Barbara Rex, Loretta Ross, and Edna and Leann Weller; Writerstable members: KT Bothwell, Dale Clem, Lue English, Jim Gardepe, Walter Glenn, Debbie Kolb, Susan Livingston, Jane Roark, Monita Soni, and Barbara Tran. Special thanks to JB's group: Jeremy Bronaugh, Paul Lees-Haley and Mike Guillebeau.

To the parishioners of Kipp Presbyterian Church.
Your loving kindness taught me important lessons
about being a pastor

May 1987
Harvest, Kansas

*p*astor Suzanne stepped into the pulpit and gripped it hard, but it failed to steady her. She scanned the small congregation, her eyes resting on one face and then another, ending with the tearful faces of her children in the back pew. During the opening Call to Worship and first hymn, the people leaned toward her as if she were a powerful magnet.

"Let us confess our sins," she said. The room grew dark pulling the small group closer to each other. On the communion table, candles gave off an uncertain light, their flames fluttering in the disturbed air.

She had seen the storm approaching earlier when she and the children left Salina. As they drove out to the country church, they saw gray clouds far out west rolling over the Kansas plains, but by the time she pulled up in front of the church, the storm was closer and darker. Purplish black clouds boiled and raged rushing toward the little church which sat in the midst of miles and miles of fields.

Soon after she began the worship service, the storm was overhead. The rain built steadily from a drumbeat to a fury and before long the pounding on the roof drowned out the songs and responses. But the people followed along as always, bowing their heads for prayer and singing the familiar words:

As it was in the beginning,
is now and ever shall be,
World without end. Amen. Amen.

Suzanne glanced down, but the fluorescent light glowed harshly on the empty pulpit. No order of worship and no sermon prompted her today. "We've journeyed far over the past months," she said, "and we've persevered through all the anguish and confusion. This week's tragedy has brought us some answers, but it has also brought grief and . . . and regret." Lightning flashed and froze the moment. Then thunder shook the room.

She raised her voice to be heard. "I keep asking myself what I could have done to prevent this dreadful death." She tried to wipe away the tears with one swipe, but they kept coming. She stopped to dry her eyes and regain her composure.

Their stricken eyes and hers connected. "My God, what have we done?" she said over the roaring wind and rain. She lowered her fist. "What have we done?"

CHAPTER 1

September 7, 1986
First Sunday

Suzanne tip-toed up the creaking stairs, each step announcing her intrusion throughout the building. She passed empty bulletin boards on the side walls and, at the top of the stairs, a thick rope hanging down from the bell tower. Taking a deep breath, she pushed open the door to the sanctuary. The sweet spice of old wood washed over her bringing back warm memories of other churches.

She had found the country church without difficulty and was early, intending to practice her sermon; however, six people were already seated here and there in the pews. Each one looked up but no one spoke as Suzanne's good morning echoed in the small room. She emptied her arms, laying her robe and sermon materials on the front pew, and approached each one to introduce herself. They shook her hand and mumbled their names.

She took deep breaths. First Sundays were always difficult for her.

The assignment to Harvest Church had come up suddenly and she had little information. Dr. Talley, the Presbytery Executive, had simply offered her to three of the church's leaders. "Consider this a gift. The other Presbyterian churches in Northern Kansas will help support Pastor Suzanne for a year. You can try to revitalize your congregation or . . . well, make decisions about the future." The elders had little to say, but they all signed the agreement.

Suzanne looked for the bulletins showing the morning's order of worship. They weren't on the piano near the door. They weren't across the room on the pulpit either. Self-conscious that every movement disturbed the silence of the early worshipers, she picked up her robe and stepped lightly across the chancel area to the tiny office set into the wall next to the choir. She found a nail behind the door to hang her robe on. Back in the main room she examined an oil painting which covered most of the front wall behind the choir chairs. A realistic, though much larger-than-life, Jesus walked a path with a flock of sheep following him out of a dark forest. He carried a lamb in his left arm and reached out his right hand. Frozen in the middle of his next step forward, he looked straight into Suzanne's eyes.

The entrance stairs creaked, and the thinnest woman she had ever seen rushed in. She walked at a forty-five degree angle from the floor and hurried to the piano bench where she emptied her arms of books and papers.

Suzanne moved to introduce herself; but when she did, the woman kept fussing with her papers and never looked up. "I'm Tess. I play for services. Here's your worship bulletin. Took me forever to print them. I had to go to my brother's store twice. Copier was broken." Tess the pianist was not only blessed with an unusual shape, she also spoke rapidly in a high-pitched whine.

One of the men she had met at the introductory meeting arrived, took the other bulletins from Tess, nodded at Suzanne without speaking and went to stand at the door. A big boned, solid woman followed him. Looming over Suzanne, she nodded toward the man holding the bulletins. "I'm Alberta, my husband's Alton. I'll do all except your scripture, sermon, prayer and benediction so you can see how we do things." Before Suzanne could say thank you, she turned to talk to a man in the front pew.

Suzanne felt like she had as a child, small and insignificant. *I wonder if it would make a difference if I were tall and male,* she thought. Her five foot two slight frame left her feeling far from authoritative, but she had never been sure if it was totally due to the way people reacted to her.

The service went fine, but it felt strange to Suzanne, bare and chilly. Alberta didn't welcome or introduce her so she did that herself. And when she was preaching she could detect little response. Their eyes were dull, their bodies stiff.

Suzanne missed her church in Columbus and its stained glass windows, pipe organ and excellent choir. Harvest's pulpit and communion table were rough hewn, and the choir area was full of small metal folding chairs. Those chairs sat empty in front of the one saving grace in the room, the painting of Jesus with the lambs.

There wasn't much conversation at the door afterward. Nobody even asked about her accent. She had tamed her southern drawl, but someone usually asked where she came from.

After the service, Tess and she were the last ones out of the building. "I'll need your sermon title by Wednesday," Tess said, "so I can type the bulletin. I'll choose the hymns to be sure they're ones we all know."

"Okay," Suzanne said, "I'm glad you'll do the typing and copying, but take this hymnal and circle all the numbers of the hymns you and the congregation know. Then I can select ones that go with the scripture and sermon of the day, and they'll also be ones you're familiar with."

"You want me to write in the hymnal?" she asked.

"Yes, this will be my worship hymnal and I'll choose hymns from it and tell you what they are by Wednesday each week."

"You sure you want me to write in the hymnal?"

CHAPTER 2

First Sunday At Home

---

*W*hen Suzanne got home her husband Bell asked, "How was your first day?" He ladled roast beef and vegetables from the slow cooker onto each plate.

"It was okay," she said, collapsing into her chair. "It's the smallest church I've ever been in."

"When can we see it? When can we go to church with you?" Peter wanted to know.

"Let me get settled a little bit first," she said.

Later, when Peter and Julie left the table, she told Bell more. "It was unlike any church I've ever been in. The people weren't very friendly, and the pulpit is so close to the pews I had to be sure I didn't talk too loud. There are only seven pews, divided by a center aisle. It's all a bit rough, and the room feels bare—barren may be a better word for it. But there is a beautiful realistic oil painting of Jesus and the Lambs."

"Have they set the date for a welcome dinner?" he asked.

"There was no mention of it. Of course, this has happened so quickly, it may take all of us a while to get up to speed."

"Well, when they do plan one, let me know so I can hold the date. Suze, I had no idea that if I took this position at First Presbyterian, nothing would be available that fits you. After you were so successful in Columbus, I assumed. . . ."

"It is a surprise how spread out the churches are in Kansas," she said. "The hardest thing for me is to have us split between two churches. It means we'll have three families: your church; my church and our family at home with Julie and Peter."

"We'll manage. We've been unusually fortunate up to now since I had no Sunday duties in Columbus and we could all be part of your church." He picked up his dishes and took them to the kitchen.

She sat at the table alone, staring into space.

CHAPTER 3

Why Me?

Suzanne backed out of the garage in Salina to drive out to the church for her first Women's Meeting. She tried to breathe deeply and relax but before she knew it her teeth were clenched again.

For four weeks she had struggled to know the people. But she still wrote sermons to unknown souls and delivered them to staring eyes. Every attempt at communication smacked up against an invisible wall. Her mind, body and soul continued searching for information, and she pled with God to help her see why she was in that place.

Previous parishioners had been strangers for only a short time before they became as close as family. *Surely, it will happen here. In a few months I'll be amazed that there was a time when these people were not part of my life.*

Her car hugged the road as she sped up to pull out of the curve on Wild Turkey Pike. Her purse and planner went sliding to the floor. "Dammit," she complained under her breath, but let them go and kept her speed steady. She rarely met any cars and only had to pause at one stop sign between her back door and the church door. So far her best time was

29 minutes. "Twenty miles, twenty-nine minutes, but galaxies apart," she said in her best TV announcer voice.

She tried to think positively about meeting with the women of the congregation, but they had been cool and distant from the start, and she felt awkward around them.

One morning her office chair wasn't at her desk. She searched through the entire building and finally found it in a basement storage closet.

"I feel like they don't want me there. Do you think I'm paranoid?" she had asked Bell that night before going upstairs to bed.

"Oh, they'll warm up," he said kissing her good night from his recliner. "You've never needed any more than a couple of sermons to win anyone over."

"Maybe so. The rural setting is new for me. It may take a while longer," she said over her shoulder starting up the stairs as he turned back to the television. "But by this time I'm usually as excited as an archaeologist on a dig. I'll keep trying to connect."

* * *

She had taken a list of questions to her first meeting with the currently elected elders, expecting to begin getting organized and together make decisions about how they would lead the church.

After an opening prayer, she asked, "What is a typical agenda for your meetings?"

"Huh, we never done that," Alton said.

"Help me know how you are organized," she said. "What committees do you all have?"

"We just do what's needed," Alton said. He was so bent over, making eye contact was difficult.

The other two men avoided looking at her. Mack sat at the end of the long table opposite Alton. He wore overalls and a John Deere cap; and he busily cleaned his yellowed, corn-like fingernails with a pocket knife. Occasionally he yawned openly but said nothing.

One elder Eva was out of town. The other one, Junior, looked alert but said nothing. He was by far the youngest member of the congregation, mid-twenties Suzanne guessed. His new jeans and white shirt were sharply creased. *He probably lives with his mother.*

She persisted with them. "This is different for me. My last church had 750 members and 20 active elders. So, I need to get used to what it's like to have 35 members and 4 elders. What do you usually do at your monthly meetings?" There was complete silence. Junior glanced up at her but quickly looked away focusing on Alton again.

"I haven't found a list of church members. I'll need that and also names of those who can't get to church, nursing home people and others who are home bound," Suzanne said.

There was no response.

After a long pause, Alton said, "Eva might know. She and George, they went off to Denver to visit their new grandbaby. Ask her." Mack and Junior continued to look at Alton but not at her. There was only one item of business. "We're gonna have to start locking the church," Alton said. "Ain't never locked it before. Don't like to see a church locked up."

"Why would you lock it now?" she asked. "Has there been trouble?"

"Gotta keep the ghosts in." Alton cackled and wheezed as he looked at the floor. He was as stooped and gnarled as an old bush.

"Tell me about the ghosts," she said.

He pivoted his head sideways and looked up at her out of his left eye. "Some things are best left quiet. All us who belong here will have keys so we can get in. But it'll keep out any mischief makers."

The stop sign at Magnolia Road brought her back to the moment. She turned left and put the accelerator on the floor. There were several miles here of good, straight pavement where she could go seventy, even eighty. A glance at the clock showed she was tied with her best time so far. She looked out over the dull, lonely fields of stubble.

Bell would be surprised at her speeding. She usually warned him to let up with his heavy foot. But he couldn't possibly comprehend what this was like for her. It only took him five minutes to get across town to his church.

But it's where they were for now. He had been called to serve First Presbyterian and she apparently had been called to Harvest Church.

The empty road provided no distraction, no other cars to play with, no searching for possible openings, and no guessing game about which lane of traffic would move most quickly.

She turned the knob back and forth on the radio. KHCC was playing violin music. It hurt her ears. The country music was twangy and sad. She certainly wasn't in the mood for rock. The oldies station was playing John Denver from another lifetime. She didn't want to think about that time right now.

She slowed down at the potholes on Magnolia Drive. At least dodging them presented some challenge to her driving ability.

They looked like Ohio potholes. She'd have thought they'd be different somehow. Her throat tightened as she thought of what she, Bell, and the children had given up to enter this foreign territory: closeness to family and friends, a thriving church family. A tear plopped on her arm. She angrily brushed it away.

Bell's decision to leave his position as Director of Social Services and go back to parish ministry had jerked them all around. Peter's response, typical for a twelve-year-old, had been, "Fine. Have a good life. I'm staying in Columbus."

Eleven-year-old Julie wasn't so angry. At least if she was it didn't show. All she said was, "I don't think it makes sense to move when all our friends are here."

"It will be good for all of us," Suzanne told them. "God doesn't just move one person in a family. This will be good for all of us." She repeated those words many times as if saying it enough would make it true. It was what her grandmother had told her when she was a child and the Air Force moved her family every year or two.

The biggest potholes stretched all the way across the road. Down into a crater she rocked and then slowly moved out, like a boat riding the waves.

When she slowed down for another gaping hole, she noticed her hands were hurting. Her fingers gripped the steering wheel so tightly that her rings were making grooves in them. She leaned back and forced herself to relax with ten deep breaths.

Remember the Prime Directive, she told herself. Captain James T. Kirk would say, "Don't interfere with their culture. Listen, listen, listen. Observe." She repeated the litany of reminders, knowing her own tendency to take charge, get people organized and make everything work "right." *No matter what they do*, she told herself, *do not take over. Listen and observe; watch and learn before you jump in to help.*

A grain elevator stood up like a church spire beyond the field to her right. That was her marker. At the next road, she turned right following the blacktop and turned right again onto the road that led into

Harvest. She drove slowly now. Sometimes children and dogs were in the road. There were none today. In fact, there was no movement at all.

Even though Dr. Talley had described Harvest as a small village, Suzanne hadn't imagined a place so small that there wasn't even a McDonald's. Boards covered the doors and windows of a little store and post office. There were a few dirt paths off the main road, several houses, a rusty relic of a gas pump, and the grain elevator facing the church.

The elevator towered over everything. Across from it, the little white church, topped with its bell tower, sat keeping watch. Train tracks ran across the road just past the elevator and the church, but she hadn't heard or seen any trains.

Suzanne pulled up in front of the church and parked next to four dust-covered cars and two trucks. Their tails stuck out into the road, and their noses angled in, pointing to the church. Her shiny red car looked out of place beside them.

She was on time. Others were early. *Relax*, she told herself, then grabbed her purse and organizer off the floor, willing herself to enter. *If you're going to be their pastor, it's time to make some connections with them.*

CHAPTER 4

The Women's Meeting

*H*er heel caught on the cracked sidewalk. Each step rang out, the only sound in this otherwise silent world.

Suzanne had dressed carefully for the meeting. When she was trying to decide what to wear the night before, her mother had called from Alabama. "Darlin', don't you wear pants whatever you do. Older women dress up for church meetings," she said.

So she chose a mint green suit with a knee length skirt, a pastel pink blouse and nail polish to match. She fixed her hair in a French twist to give herself more height. Every detail was carefully considered, but such decisions had become difficult. Her proper upbringing couldn't help her in rural Kansas.

The sun warmed her skin while the wind blew in hints of fall. It was unnaturally quiet, no humming of motors, no traffic, no sounds of children or dogs. Not even the wind made a sound. It never stopped blowing though, and today it blew straight into her back, forceful yet silent.

Near the road, a white wooden sign hung from its frame. Its squeak broke the silence now and then as it swung back and forth. The former pastor's name was so faded no one could read it from the road.

Suzanne went around the side of the church to the basement door instead of entering through the double doors which led directly upstairs. As she stepped in, a wave of heat and the smell of gas surrounded her.

She took the steep stairs to the lower level and passed the bright white kitchen. She heard voices around the corner in the meeting room.

At the far end, seven women huddled in a tight semicircle around a gas heater. There were no seats left so Suzanne said a soft "Hello," took a folding chair from against the wall and carried it over to the group. No one moved to expand the huddle so she sat behind them, glad to have a row of chairs and bodies between her and the heat. The women were deep into a conversation.

"Got to dry up so we can drill wheat."

"Jensen put his in already."

She wondered if somehow no one had noticed her entering. She felt invisible and wished she were. Her suit was neon in this setting. One of the women wore sweat pants, a couple had on house dresses; the others, jeans and sweatshirts.

They went on talking about the wheat. Suzanne noticed tables set up in the middle of the room. Otherwise everything was the same as when she had examined it the first week. The oak cupboards and beige indoor-outdoor carpeting looked new. The whole building was clean and well-kept. There was an old Cradle Roll attendance banner on one wall and under it an ancient safe which stood open. She had inspected its contents: three old hymnals, a letter over forty years old from the Presbytery congratulating the church on its mission giving in 1945, attendance folders from various years gone by, and a few old Sunday School books. She recognized <u>A Promise to Keep</u> and <u>God's World and Johnny</u> from her own early years. That was all there was in the room except tables and chairs folded up against the walls next to several portable dividers.

The conversation had turned from the wheat to someone who was sick. She opened her planner ready to make notes; but before she could ask for a name, Alberta said, "Yep, it's a good thing you got the vet out right away." Suzanne renewed her determination to be cautious in this foreign land. *Listen and observe. Listen and observe,* her internal mantra continued.

She had previously met five of the seven women. Eva sat straight across on the other side of the half circle of chairs. She had been absent from the first Board of Elders meeting; and as the others had indicated, she was indeed the one with information. When Eva stopped in the church office to bring flowers in honor of her new grandchild, Suzanne asked her for the names and locations of members and an indication of those who were nursing home residents.

Eva had rattled off their names. "I'll have to make a list and sketch you a map of where the others live. None of the roads have signs. Everybody knows where everybody's land is because most of it's been in our families for generations." She reminded Suzanne of an executive secretary, efficient and distant. Her eyes squinted and stared up at the wall as she retrieved facts and dispensed them.

That day her charcoal hair, streaked with mahogany, hung in one long braid down her back. It was still braided for the women's meeting but instead of hanging down her back, it wound around the top of her head. *If I were an artist,* Suzanne thought, *I'd paint her picture in oils just to try to capture that hair.*

When she finished talking to one of the two women Suzanne didn't know, Eva looked up and nodded in a greeting. Suzanne relaxed a little.

Between Eva and the stove slumped Minnie. Her pink scalp showed through thin white hair. *Maybe that's why she always wears a man's hat to church,* Suzanne thought.

Minnie had a spooky voice that sounded like a train whistle in the distance. "Youu knoow, I liike church," she had said to Suzanne the previous Sunday. Occasionally her eyes twinkled mischievously, but today Minnie's cloudy blue eyes stared at the stove the way they stared at the picture of Jesus and the lambs on Sundays. Suzanne had heard someone call her Minnie Mouse and noticed the delight wash over her face at hearing the nickname.

On the near side of the stove and to Suzanne's right was Tess the pianist. Suzanne had a perfect view of her in profile, her triangle of a nose, tiny and tilted, and age lines which emphasized her mouth's permanent sneer. A scar pulled the left side up slightly. Suzanne reminded herself that the sneer didn't necessarily reflecting Tess's feelings. However, her words and reactions often did match her face. Her voice did, too. Squeaky as a poorly played violin, it peeled Suzanne's nerves. Everything she said sounded like a whine as that mouth sneered and that nose pointed. This woman of sixty-something, built like a junior high school girl, sounded like a perpetually unhappy young teen.

"I've been real busy," she said when Suzanne asked about the hymnbook she was going to mark. "That hymnbook isn't my top priority."

Directly in front of Suzanne was Bertha, someone she looked forward to knowing better. She had made a couple of insightful comments about her sermons - the only comments anyone had made.

Bertha reminded Suzanne of her grandmother. She had the same gentle, blue eyes. Suzanne admired her hair as she stared at her soft, round back. Until now, gray had been gray unless it was tinted blue or pink. Seeing them all together, Suzanne noticed the shades of gray. Bertha's was the shine and color of a new stainless steel pan. It was soft on the sides and pulled into a doughnut on the back of her head. Suzanne's grandmother used to wear her hair like that, and she wished she'd asked how she made it into a doughnut when she was alive. Some day if she got to know her well enough, she'd ask Bertha.

Alberta, the leader who wasn't leading, sat in the middle of the half circle, furthest from the stove. On her left and right were the two women Suzanne didn't know. Alberta didn't engage in dialogue; she made pronouncements, this time about dates for wheat planting. It was difficult to ever ignore her. If her imposing size didn't command notice, her loud, demanding voice would. Its full bass was rough, and it carried over everything else like a horn on a truck.

In contrast to Alton her bent twig of a husband, Alberta looked like an oak tree. Her coarse gray hair was the color of a battleship. She had a no-nonsense cut, straight around from ear to ear with bangs down to her eyebrows.

Alberta hadn't yet called the meeting to order, a surprise since she was so in charge all the time. Even at the elders meeting Alberta had been present in spirit. Alton prefaced most of his comments with, "As my wife says. . . ."

The women around the gas stove hunched toward each other and began talking about someone whose daughter was in the hospital. Suzanne's head began to ache. If she were home, she could be fixing supper and working on Sunday's sermon.

Alberta said, "She had a tumor the size of a grapefruit. Never heard of such a thing." Suzanne wondered how they could stand the heat. She kept wiping her upper lip and finally slipped off her suit jacket and hung it over the back of her chair.

She was waiting for a chance to ask if this was someone for her to call on in the hospital when she noticed that her breathing was shallow and fast. No doubt some was from anxiety and some from the air being so thick with the gas heat. Suddenly, they all stopped talking and looked at her. They just looked. No one said anything. She wondered what she had missed. Maybe she had gasped aloud.

Suzanne introduced herself to those she hadn't met and acknowledged each of the others with a smile and a nod. "I'm glad to get to know you all better and see what you do." Minnie and Tess huddled on either side of the stove and stared at it. Eva looked for something in her purse, but Bertha turned around and smiled, and Alberta nodded.

No one said anything for a moment and then Tess broke in, "Bertha, Grady and I were talking about Ellen this morning at breakfast and wondering how she's getting along since her move back here from Washington."

While Bertha was answering her, Suzanne glanced at her watch. They were already twenty minutes late. Wasting time, starting late, and no clear agenda were pet peeves of hers. It looked like they were in for all three. Alberta still showed no sign of getting things going. *Oh, Lord, that list of mine for today won't get done if we don't get this meeting over with.*

The women droned on and on about people she didn't know. Suzanne was about to force the issue by asking what their usual meeting format was when Tess whined, "When are we getting to the quilting?"

"Wait," Alberta ordered. "First things first." She began a business meeting which was a parody of parliamentary procedure. Discussions meandered from their balance in the checking account to the next event, an annual chicken noodle supper.

Suzanne was surprised to hear that they had a checkbook balance of $3000. "Do you have special missions you support," she asked. They looked blank so she tried again. "What do you use your money for?" she asked.

Finally, Alberta said rather sharply, "We use it for whatever's needed."

In the discussion of the chicken noodle supper it became clear that the quilt played some part. "Is it a door prize?" Suzanne asked. They didn't know what she meant. "Do you mean that everyone buys a ticket for dinner and then one of those tickets is drawn to find out who wins the quilt?"

"Why that wouldn't work!" Tess said, turning that triangle of a nose until it pointed accusingly at Suzanne.

Bertha turned around in her chair and said, "Pastor Suzanne, you come see for yourself. We've been doing this for as long as I can remember so it's hard for us to describe it. You'll see for yourself. It's always the first Wednesday in December."

"Okay," Suzanne said. "How can I help? Do you all sell tickets? Shall I bake something?"

Alberta opened her purse and handed her ten $3.00 tickets for dinner and ten $1.00 tickets for the quilt. "You can bring two pies."

Bertha asked them to move to a long table where she passed out Bibles. The lesson was short. They took turns reading the passage about Jesus being tempted in the desert wilderness for forty days and forty nights. Then all eyes were on Bertha. In her gentle way, voice mellow and soothing, she pointed out that forty days means it was a long time.

"We don't know exactly how long it was. But we do know it was a difficult time. Jesus searched his soul to decide what he was going to do. Would he use his power to feed people, would he use it to be saved by angels after jumping off a tall building? That way he could convince people that he was sent by God. Would he do whatever it took to gain all the kingdoms of the world as his own so he could force people do what he wanted? He had some right difficult choices to make, don't you know?

"I expect we've all been through such times when it seemed like we were in a desert or a wilderness," she said, her soothing voice rising and falling with her bosom as though she were rocking them and singing a lullaby. "Remember a time when you weren't sure which way to turn. Maybe your life was all upside down." She paused, eyes closed, face serene. "That's what you could call your time in the desert or the wilderness. You didn't know how to do it, but you had to make decisions. And choices about how to follow God weren't clear.

"Some of those choices would lead to good and some would lead to evil. Jesus decided none of the three possibilities tempting him were right. He chose another way. We'll study that next time."

There was no discussion, but Bertha went to the heart of it as it applied to the women in the group.

She was glad that there was no deferring to her as pastor, no self-consciousness in Bertha. She made no disclaimer about not being a scholar, nor did she ask the pastor questions to reassure herself she was on target. This was good. A small church like this with a frequent turnover of pastors would die without their lay leaders.

Bertha closed the study time with an honest prayer. Her words were those of one accustomed to talking with God as a friend. She included the names of many who were ill or in difficulty and even Susie, the ailing cow. When she finished, there were tears in some eyes and tissues surreptitiously brought out.

Suzanne wondered what their wilderness times had been.

Eva and Alberta brought the quilt out from behind a wooden divider where it stood on the ends of its frame. They removed a plastic drop cloth and placed the quilt over two of the long tables set side to side. They were the kind of tables found in most church basements, six feet long with legs that fold up, wooden tops scratched, dented, scraped, stained, and crayoned from many human encounters. Suzanne had never before been with a group of women who quilted, but she knew those tables.

Tess complained as she rummaged in the cabinet for scissors, "Things are moved around and I can never find anything in the church." She pulled out a thick leather book. "Well, what's this doing here?"

"I'll be," Alberta said. After a long moment in which they all stared at the book, Alberta told Suzanne, "It's an old record book that's been missing for several years. We'd given up looking for it."

Merciful heavens," Bertha said, "why do you suppose it would be there? I'm sure it wasn't here last month when we cleaned. That cabinet was my job."

Knowing looks passed around the group. "Must be our ghost," Minnie said quietly. She was hunched over the quilt, putting in tiny stitches even though her eyes looked unfocused.

Soon everyone was seated around the quilt and into a rhythm. Needles were pushed down and pulled up, down and up. Suzanne was glad her grandmother had taught her how to do this. She was more comfortable and relaxed with something to occupy her—and with more distance from the stove. Quilting made her feel like part of the group though she was quite aware she was not. The conversation and easy quiet rose and fell with the stitches.

"Grady had to call the vet in, can't let it get to his precious bulls."

"Our set-aside's hard to figure this year."

"We got to do some more terracing to get in the program."

"Homer's having a hard time turning his ground, still too wet."

Some of what they talked about was hard for Suzanne to follow, but she didn't break the rhythm by asking questions.

Bertha mentioned a family which had recently moved nearby, "Out to the old Jones place. I understand they have five little children, and I thought we could see if they want to come to church. We could have a Sunday School again."

"I already checked on that," Eva said. "They're Catholic and go into town."

There were sounds of disappointment around the tables. "We used to have 70 children here on Sunday mornings," Tess said in her little voice.

"And we had that many in Christian Endeavor on Sunday nights, too," said Laura, one of the women Suzanne had met that day. "We had some good times."

"Where have all the people gone?" Minnie sang in her cracked voice.

There was silence for a few minutes, and then Suzanne said, "Tell me more about this ghost of yours."

Bertha was sitting next to her and after a lengthy pause she spoke in her soft and gentle voice. "One Saturday, Tess brought the white communion cloth over and put it on the table. The next morning when we came in for church, it was wadded up under the choir chairs."

Tess repeated the story, adding her own details, "I took the cloth home to treat the stains, grape juice, don't you know, hard to get out. I washed it. I ironed it. It's not the easiest thing in the world to iron. I put it on the communion table. The next morning I found it in a heap on the floor."

"We figured some kids was fooling around. That's why we put the lock on the door," Alberta said and quickly asked who wanted coffee and who wanted tea. Eva refused any refreshment; and while the others gathered back around the stove, she kept working on the quilt.

Minnie fussed about cream and sugar. "I cleeean fergot to bring any. I can go hoome and get some. It will oonly take a minute. Want some creeam in your coffee? I can go get some."

Bertha managed to distract her. "I declare, Minnie, you make the best banana bread there ever was. You know, even when I make it by your recipe, it never tastes this good. What's your secret?"

"Youu could try real butter, unsalted; that could make a difference."

Suzanne asked for the recipe. Minnie grinned and said she'd bring it on Sunday. "It's different from any other recipe for it that I've seen," she whispered, looking at Suzanne with mischief in her eyes. "It's made with biscuit mix. Don't tell anybody."

As they cleaned up to leave, Suzanne told Alberta that she was taking the record book home, giving her no chance to object, then moved to help Eva cover the quilt with the plastic and stand it between the divider and the wall. "Sure hope nothing happens to this," Eva whispered.

She looked around. They were the last to leave. Keeping her voice low, she said, "Here are the maps. Don't tell anybody I did them for you. Some think I try to run the church, especially, when I try to get them organized."

They joined the others on the sidewalk outside the door. Tess turned to Suzanne and pointed at a sharp metal object on the ground to one side of the door. "Know what this is?" she asked Suzanne. It had been embedded in cement and looked like it had been there at least as long as the cracked sidewalk. Suzanne had never seen anything like it. It resembled an upside down ice skate blade, rusty and dangerous. A child might fall on it. Of course, there were no children in the church now.

"It's where the men scrape their boots," Tess said. "This is farm country."

It sounded like a warning or a not so subtle way of saying "you don't belong here."

As she backed her car out into the road, Suzanne noticed the others were still standing on the sidewalk talking.

CHAPTER 5

To Stay or Not to Stay

*O*n her way back through the potholes, Suzanne began to think. *How can I get out of this commitment? If it's a call from God, the people sure don't confirm it.*

At home, the questions in her mind persisted. She stood in the kitchen cutting up broccoli and carrots for a stir fry. "I'm having trouble getting hold of what to do there," she told Bell. She had to raise her voice every time he disappeared into the next room with plates and glasses. "Finally, I have their names and maps to their homes. Usually, I'd try to get them organized; but they do things so differently that I'm not sure that's what's most needed."

"What do you think about that ghost they've mentioned?" Bell asked.

"Oh, it's children playing in there, I imagine. Yesterday when I went in, the pulpit chairs were upside down behind the last pew. One Sunday the choir chairs were all folded up – not that it matters. There is no choir to sit there, but the chairs are usually open and in place. My books are sometimes moved, and I found the pulpit Bible in the basement last Sunday."

"You could end up spending all your time and energy dealing with that."

"I know. That's what I don't want to happen. Of course, they need to resolve that ghost business; but truthfully I think it gives them something to talk about. They may be disappointed if it stops. But there's a lock on the door now so that should put a stop to it.

"What bothers me most is how hard it is to get acquainted in a meaningful way. They . . . avoid me. It's hard to feel called by God to such an empty, perfunctory ministry."

"Are you wondering if you've been recalled?" he said. "Remember Professor Sims telling us, 'Don't get too comfortable. God calls but God can also re-call.'"

"You mean like no longer called to the ministry?" she asked.

"I'm not saying that's what's going on. I'm just wondering if you think so. This is way different from football, but when I was on the bench too much, I began to feel it wasn't my thing to do." Bell lifted the wok from an overhead cupboard.

"I've never doubted my calling. Have you?"

"You loved working with the congregation in Columbus even when it was a dysfunctional mess. And it was amazing how you turned it around."

"Hmmm," she said.

"Harvest is a waste of your abilities. In fact, I'm insulted that you would even be asked to go there. You have so much to offer. You should leave now before you get attached and they drag you down under their problems. I'm going to talk to Dr. Talley about it. The presbytery should have arranged a suitable job for you when they called me here."

"No, don't do that. I can handle it. I'll ask him to help me understand what's going on. And he'll know if another church is opening up. But I have to be prepared if nothing else becomes available."

"Well, Suze, I sure could use your help at First Church. If you come work with me until something else comes along, you could really make a difference. Maybe you could head up our Healthy Living Outreach to the community. We have funds and there are people in need of food and medical care, but we need a good organizer for it. And they liked your preaching when you filled in last month. We could arrange some preaching, too."

Yes, she could volunteer at Bell's church, be his right hand woman. He'd like that and his congregation had made it clear they'd like her to be there.

On the other hand, those first weeks when she was helping him get started in his church, going to every activity, she felt like a spare kidney, an adjunct to him, not necessary but good to have around. And she had to be sure not to overshadow him when she preached. She didn't want to affect the confidence his congregation put in him or give an opportunity for the people to choose up sides.

"We'll see, Bell. I'll talk to Dr. Talley when he gets back from vacation."

After dinner, Suzanne took a long, hot bath. The house was quiet. Bell had a meeting. Peter was studying at a friend's house. Julie was in her room, having requested not to be distracted from her "piles of homework." Suzanne wondered when they had started doing their homework without arguing.

She was glad to be alone after a day of confusing contacts with the people of Harvest Church and the conversation with Bell on top of that. The hot water pressed upon tight muscles and demanded they relax. Her headache began to ease. Finally, her mind followed, slowing to a manageable pace and familiar rhythm.

When she curled up in bed with the record book found at the church that morning, she found nothing of interest. It was full of hand-written minutes of meetings dated 1960 to 1970 that simply recorded actions of the elders: births, deaths, communion served, and several members' transfers to other churches.

Putting that aside, Suzanne picked up her writing book, a simple school notebook. In times like this when she had so much to think about, scribbling a while released some of the thoughts. It made sleeping easier because it was more probable that she wouldn't have "working dreams." She was blessed and cursed with vivid dreams which often left her tired physically and emotionally.

She wrote fast and without the need to meet any requirements. She wrote her prayers, the names of people she'd met that day, questions she wanted to ask, sermon ideas. Then she made a list for the following day. First she would pick up the hymnal Tess had promised to have ready.

I might yet find some reason I've been called to Harvest. Who knows, this ghost of theirs may be someone in desperate need of love and attention.

CHAPTER 6

Tess and Grady

*D*espite anxious dreams about getting lost, she had no trouble finding Tess and Grady's house. Eva's map led her two miles down a gravel road to the white house with yellow trim. It sat alone in the middle of flat land that spread out for miles of muddy gray stubble. A white barn hovered behind the house, but no other buildings were within sight. Suzanne pulled in behind a pick up truck covered with mud.

On the front porch a gold and white collie looked at her kindly. And when she knocked, Tess quickly opened the door. The dog followed them in. She was almost as big as Tess, but she picked her up and carried her outside. "Damn dog is always in the way," she said.

In the living room dark furniture with curlicues and carvings sat heavy in the room. A proud silver tea set and white lace napkins on the coffee table caught Suzanne's attention. She wondered if Tess was expecting someone else.

"I asked Grady to come in and meet you, but he's busy out in the barn." She picked up the teapot and disappeared through a door.

I don't mind going out there," Suzanne called after her.

"That would get him in here. Nobody is allowed in the barn, he doesn't want anybody to see his art."

Suzanne looked around the room for a clue to what that art was. One large landscape hung over the couch, and there were a few stitched samplers.

When Tess returned, Suzanne asked about Grady's art. "Oh, you won't find any in here!" Tess sneered. "Oh,no, no, no. Those disgusting paintings stay in the barn."

"Whaa-?" Suzanne started to ask.

Tess interrupted. "Animals, all animals. Well, here we are now. Here's your tea and here's the hymnal. I marked the ones we all know and like. It took me three evenings." Suzanne thanked her and quickly chose the hymns for Sunday so she would know what to practice.

When Tess jumped up and pointed to pictures on top of an old upright piano, Suzanne tried to follow the rapid fire introduction to her family. "Our daughter Sarah is a hospice nurse. She never stays in one place very long. And our son Sam studies graphic design in Tulsa. They never come home."

Tess's parents stood stiffly all in black in front of stone columns. "They died years ago in an accident, not too long after Grady and I married. And these are Grady's parents." A stocky man stood with his hands resting on his wife's shoulders; both were grinning. "They lived in this house until his mother died and his father went into a nursing home. That's when we tore down the old home place over on the other side of the barn and moved in here."

She pointed to a row of dog pictures. "Grady's, all collies, all named Lassie," Tess said. "When one dies he gets another. But this one acts like she's my dog, follows me everywhere; and I don't even like dogs. Grady spoils her. I swear he'd sleep with her if I'd allow it."

Finally, someone was talking to her. "I'd like to meet Grady and see his paintings," Suzanne said.

Tess jerked her head up quickly, "He'd have a fit if I –."

The back door slammed. Grady was over six foot tall with intense blue eyes and thick, coal black hair. He hung his head down, took his cap off, and grinned, "Ah, the lady pastor." He shook her hand. Paint splattered his overalls; his boots looked ancient and comfortable.

"Grady, I'm glad to meet you. I see you sneaking into church late and leaving early." She teased him and he smiled. "Tell me, what's this mysterious art work of yours?"

"Aw, I fool around with drawing animals, they're just for myself. Animals are my whole life. I feed and water them, call the vet when they're sick, keep them safe. And I make pictures of them."

Tess interrupted, "The best thing he's ever done was the painting for church, the one of Jesus and the sheep."

"You did that?" Suzanne asked. "It's extraordinary. Would you let me see your other work?"

Tess interrupted again, "Oh, no! They're not what you think."

Grady opened his mouth to speak then closed it. Without another word, he simply turned and went back through the kitchen, slamming the back door.

Oh, he's not just being modest or shy, Suzanne thought. *Maybe he paints nudes. But hadn't they said "animals?"*

"Have you been to see Bertha?" Tess asked. "She's been feeling poorly."

Suzanne felt dismissed. "Tell me, Tess, would she expect a call before I visit or are people around here okay with the pastor just dropping in?"

"Don't ask me," she said. "You're the minister."

Breathing deeply and counting to herself, one, two, three, Suzanne said, "Well, I'll just stop over there on my way back." She made her exit as soon as she could, covering her anger and nervousness with small talk at the door and then backing out, almost stepping on the dog.

"Lassie, get off the porch!" Tess yelled.

Lassie looked serene as though she were used to ignoring the nagging voice. Suzanne stopped to pet her.

CHAPTER 7

Bertha

*S*uzanne found Bertha's farmhouse in the middle of a field off the blacktop. She pulled around to the back of the house just as Bertha was closing a gate on chickens pecking in the dirt. She was by the car before Suzanne's feet touched the ground, smiling and wiping her hands on her white apron.

"Bertha," Suzanne said, "are you feeling okay? Tess said you were under the weather."

"Tess said that? Don't know what gave her such a notion. Guess I'd better take my temperature. Come on in." She held the screen door open.

Suzanne was again reminded of her grandmother when she saw the back porch filled with sacks of feed, cleaning equipment and neat rows of Mason jars. She recognized green beans, peaches and something red, maybe beets.

Bertha led the way, and the screened door slammed behind them as they entered the warm embrace of her kitchen and the promising aroma of something baking. "Come, sit down, cup of tea?" Suzanne sat down at the round oak table, and Bertha put the kettle on. She put apple-shaped place mats in front of them and set down delicate china plates and cups.

"You wouldn't turn down a piece of apple pie would you?" She peeked in the oven. "My daughter Ellen picked some Jonathans at an orchard over near Lawrence."

"My lucky day," Suzanne said. "Sure smells good."

Bertha sat down, hands resting on her apron-covered roundness, her eyes full of goodness and humor. "Now, tell me, what did Tess say?"

"She asked if I'd been to see you, said you were feeling poorly."

"Hmmm," Bertha looked up to the ceiling. "Let's see. I've been feeling just fine. What could she be thinking? I haven't seen her since Sunday. Sometimes she – ever since Billy died – did she tell you? "

"Billy? I don't think so."

"Well, Billy was five, their first son. Grady was on the tractor, and the boy ran out. Good heavens, it was awful . . . terrible." She paused to take the pie out of the oven and pour steaming water into their cups.

"It's extra sad, too, since years before that Grady's brother also died in a tractor accident. He was 12, Grady was 14. Farming's dangerous work. Anyway, ever since Billy died, Grady doesn't talk much. He comes and helps set up at church for dinners and funerals; and he's there Sundays, but he usually arrives late and leaves early. I hear he spends most of his time in the barn with his animals and his painting."

"Oh, Bertha, I don't know how anyone could ever get over such a thing."

"My Lord, I don't guess they ever have; but, you know, farmers around here seem to be able to go on no matter what happens. When a crop fails, we don't let ourselves think about it. We just start planning for the next season. When we can't get the wheat planted, we don't fight the weather, just get up every morning and look out the window and make our plans. We learn to take what comes, I guess. But that's not to say it's easy.

"And it sure hasn't been easy for Tess and Grady," she went on. "Merciful heavens, they've had more than their share of tragedy so if Tess says something like she did about me being ill or if Grady stays off to himself, I just figure they're needing to be alone."

"Oh my," Suzanne said. "I didn't realize that what I was seeing was grief." She bit her lip. It was a lesson hard to learn: Underneath irritating behavior usually lies great pain.

"I could just shoot whoever is doing things like messing up that communion cloth after Tess did all that work getting it ready. I don't understand why anyone would want to hurt her and Grady. Of course, it's not all directed at them, but . . . well, they sure get most of the aggravation."

"How long ago did their boy die?"

"Oh, it's been over twenty years, mid 60's, but I guess Grady will never get over it. I've wondered if he feels somehow responsible for his brother's death as well as Billy's though he's never said anything like that, and he really wasn't to blame for either one. Then his mother died about, let's see, must be ten or so years after Billy, and Grady had been real close to her."

Bertha set down two pieces of pie whose golden crust barely contained the steaming apples. Its fragrance wrapped the two women together. She went on, "It's just so sad especially since he's the most tenderhearted soul I've ever met. He loves his animals, names every one of them. And he won't kill anything, not even cattle. I think that's why he chose to breed and sell bulls. It seems to me his animals and painting pictures and his faith have helped him heal some. And then, of course, there's their daughter Sarah and son Samuel. Grady is real proud of them. He perks up a lot when they come home."

"This is delicious," Suzanne said. "Tell me, Bertha, have you seen Grady's art work? He wouldn't show it to me. I thought he was being shy, but then, I guess it was a mistake for me to ask more than once."

"I've heard he's still painting, but I don't know anybody who's seen it except maybe Tess and their children. Of course, we all love his Jesus and the Lambs. He painted it when he was in college, did it especially for the church. I think of that little lamb Jesus is carrying like it was one or another of us, whoever has the latest misfortune. It has been a great comfort to me, and I think it's been a comfort to Grady."

"Ah," Suzanne said. "And do you have family, Bertha?"

"Yes," her face softened, "two girls and a boy. They moved away like most of our children, but they come see me all the time. Susie lives in Wichita. Mark is in Colorado. And my eldest, Ellen, lives in Salina. She's a doctor, an internist. She divorced last year and moved back here from Washington State with Mary, my only grandchild." She shook her head as she carried their plates to the sink. "You'll see them at church some times. Of course, with a doctor's schedule it's difficult to be regular."

Bertha went on, telling about her husband Bob who had been gone 20 years. "He died on Easter Sunday, only 62. Had lung problems, probably from pesticides we used on the farm. Nobody wore masks when he was a boy. He worked at the elevator, too - lots of dust."

Bertha insisted Suzanne take one of the pies home for her family, then stood in the door and waved goodbye as Suzanne turned the car around.

The crunching of the tires on gravel gave way to the hum of smooth blacktop. All the way home the smell of apple pie from the back seat and the warmth of Bertha's presence stayed with her even though an awareness of grief and tragedy lurked in the back of her mind.

CHAPTER 8

Alberta and Alton

The house belonged on a southern plantation. White pillars framed a wraparound porch on the ground floor and a balcony above. Beside massive doors, black marble urns overflowed with golden mums and trailing vines. A wicker rocking chair sat at the extreme left and another at the extreme right of the porch.

The sun shone brightly on a meager weedy lawn which ended where fields began. While other countryside sprouted stubble, here newly tilled soil stretched for miles; and in places tiny green shoots popped up in parallel lines.

Suzanne half expected a butler to come to the door with a mint julep, but it was Alberta who opened it. She wore polished tennis shoes and a white blouse tucked into a plaid, pleated skirt. With her Dutch boy haircut she looked like a school girl in uniform. No, she was too tall to be a school girl. Suzanne smiled. She looked like a fullback dressed as a school girl.

Following Alberta into the kitchen, she noticed the aroma of fresh baked bread; but back in the hall with mugs of coffee, the odor of Pine-Sol permeated the air. Alberta led her to the back of the house where Alton sat on a glass-enclosed porch.

He wore his usual overalls and leaned back in a recliner, reading a farm journal. He looked up and closed the journal but kept his finger marking the page. It was unusual to see his front side. Most of the time all anyone saw was his rounded back and the top of his head. He looked tired, thin skin sagged under his eyes. His chest sank into his waist.

"Who've you been to see?" Alton asked as the women sat down on overstuffed chairs facing him.

Suzanne was no stranger to the politics of a congregation and people wondering who was favored by the pastor. She answered carefully, "I've begun visiting members of the congregation, Tess yesterday and she indicated Bertha wasn't feeling well so I stopped there, too. But," she hurried on, "Bertha is okay."

Alton stared at her hard, "Did you tell either of them you was coming here?"

"No, why?" Suzanne hoped she wasn't stepping into a mine field.

"We've had a million calls this morning. Whoever it is just calls and hangs up, calls and hangs up. It's enough to make me back off of ever doing anything else for the church."

"What do the calls have to do with the church?"

"That's when they come," Alton said sitting half way up in his chair and waving his magazine for emphasis. "Anytime one of us does something extra at church or gets noticed, that's when we start getting calls."

"Have you had them traced?"

"Nah, it's not that simple out here. We don't have phones like in town. Except for the churches and the bank over in Gypsum, everybody's on a party line. The phone company can come out and try to trace a call, but they sure don't like to. See, even if they get some results, it could be anybody on that line. And to find which line is used, somebody from the phone company has got to come out here and sit in that little building up where you turn to go to Gypsum. They gotta sit there a long time. We did it once, and it didn't get us no where. Seems like the calls got even worse. And we can't just leave the phone off the hook — somebody on our line might have an emergency." He coughed a couple of times and then began uncontrollable coughing and gagging. Alberta helped him out of the chair and supported him until it was over.

"We should talk about something else," she said.

Suzanne reluctantly let it go and changed the subject. "I'm visiting every member of the congregation to get acquainted. Tell me about yourselves."

Alberta said, "Mama died when I was quite young. I took care of my dad and helped run the dairy farm."

Alton tilted his recliner back and took in ragged breaths. "This is a second marriage for me," he wheezed. "My wife died long time ago. Me and Alberta, we knowed each other since, well since forever. Her great granddaddy and mine homesteaded this land together."

Alberta took over again, "When daddy died, we married, combined our land, and built this house."

"Lots of folks was angry." Alton grinned. "See we ended up with the biggest farm in the county and the best land." Alton coughed, then waved his magazine at the fields beyond the window. "See how that wheat's sprouting? Hardly nobody's got theirs showing yet. Most land's still too wet to plant.

"We worked hard all our lives," he said, "never bought any of them fancy combines with air conditioning and radios and soft seats. That's the folks going belly up and talking about a farm crisis."

"We've worked hard and God's been good to us." Alberta said.

"We're the ends of our families. Used to be so many of us. I don't know how it could be. When we pass on . . . ." Alton choked up; and all three of them turned at the sound of an airplane flying over, to look out the porch windows. The sun was hidden now behind clouds.

Suzanne was moved by seeing Alton's shell crack. *Maybe I should say something pastoral,* she thought. *This is when some people quote scripture, but it might sound like "stuff the emotions and cheer up."* Silence seemed best. They looked out at the land and sky which extended as far as she could see and met each other way out west.

Alberta left and returned with the coffee pot. Suzanne sipped hers, enjoying the warmth of the mug in her cold hands. "I'm trying to get to know the church, but I'm really puzzled about the tablecloth incident and the phone calls. What do you think is going on?"

"I got my opinions," Alberta said. "Got my suspicions, but I don't go roun talkin about em." She finished her coffee with a big gulp and changed the subject to farming and weather. Suzanne learned that milo was a plant she'd thought was corn and that the wheat was planted in the fall to winter over and be harvested in late spring.

"What does it mean, 'drilling wheat'?" Suzanne asked.

They both chuckled. "That just means planting it," Alton said. Suzanne was sure that this conversation would be repeated with much laughter.

Soon after that, she started her getaway. "Well, I'd better be on my way. Peter and Julie will be getting home soon."

Alberta walked her to the door, then disappeared into the kitchen. "Wait just a minute. I made bread this morning. Take a loaf to your family."

CHAPTER 9

First Presbyterian Church Salina

*O*n Saturday Suzanne sat at a table in Bell's office waiting for him to finish a phone call before taking her to lunch. They had two hours before the meeting of Presbyterian Women from churches across Northern Kansas.

His office arrangement had turned out to be comfortable even after removing the couch and easy chairs. The new round table and office chairs she'd helped him pick out were more in keeping with the trend away from "too cozy." It was still friendly but more professional without going all the way back to talking across the desk to a parishioner. The property committee had also cut a small window into the door following the latest advice about protection from the onslaught of sexual harassment lawsuits.

His collection of little bells sat on one of the book shelves begging to be arranged. She began lining them up, from the smallest, only a quarter inch in diameter, to the largest which wouldn't sit on the shelf but hung from a hook screwed into the end of the shelf above. His mother, proud of her ancestry, had named him Béla, the name of four Hungarian kings; and he had been called Bell from an early age. Early in his ministry a parishioner cleverly brought him a bell from a trip to Scotland, "a bell for Bell," and from then on parishioners who wanted to give him a gift often added to his collection. She turned from arranging them as he hung up the phone.

"Chinese?" he asked. She was not surprised. He had quickly established his favorite restaurant in town.

* * *

The hostess seated them quickly at the Beijing Café. Bell was already known there. "Mr. Reverend, please, this way, please."

The aroma of Jasmine tea and the murmuring of people surrounded them. Suzanne felt her shoulders relax.

"Are you nervous about your presentation?" she asked.

"No, I'm ready." He tapped his temple. "It's all right here." As usual he hadn't written anything down. He would speak from off the top of his head.

It was the first thing his parishioners told people. "He preaches without any notes," they would brag.

"Tell me," he said, "how's it going out in the country?"

"Fortunately, when I'm in their homes, they're more talkative." She described the visits to Tess and Grady, Bertha, Alton and Alberta. "But there is something peculiar going on. They talk about annoying phone calls and the communion tablecloth that had been neatly cleaned and pressed found wadded up on the floor. I think they need a detective, not a pastor."

When she finished describing what she had observed, he said, "Get out of there. Mark my words. You need to get out of there."

The waitress brought hot and sour soup, and each sipped a spoonful. "We can figure out another way to save for college," he said. "Come back and be a volunteer at First Church. Your gifts would certainly be more useful there."

She thought for a moment. "I've been thinking about that. I'd sure like for our family to be in one church. But I think you and I would drive each other crazy. I'd want everything overly organized and you'd want to fly by the seat of your pants. And . . . , well, um." She grinned mischievously. "I'd have to be careful not to do anything better than you."

He laughed. "Never gonna happen. Okay, okay, sounds like you're feeling called to be out there."

"Well, not called to be there but I guess not sure I'm called to leave," she said as the waitress set down their Kung Pao Chicken and round balls of white rice. Bell poured hot sauce on his, but it was just right for Suzanne, spicy but tamed by the rice.

Later Bell said, "I've been to a couple of meetings with a local clergy group. They asked me to invite you to come to the next meeting. It's Monday at one. Why don't you come see if it's a good support group for you? Maybe they will have some insight about people in this area."

"Oh, I don't know. Do they do more than complain about their churches?"

"They do some problem solving but no, not really complaining. I think you'd like them. They are prayerful and supportive."

"I have an appointment with Dr. Talley at the Presbytery office that morning to talk about the church, but I'm sure I'll be finished by noon. Thanks."

* * *

At the women's meeting Suzanne drank in the music of dozens of voices harmonizing, "Joyful, joyful, we adore thee." First Presbyterian's pipe organ filled the room and led a crescendo of praise. The stained glass window at the front showed the women at the empty tomb, and those on the sides showed vignettes of biblical stories. She relaxed.

Bell's presentation about the challenges to the Presbyterian Church (USA) in the last twelve years of the twentieth century was thought-provoking though a bit too long and rambling. It was the risk he took when speaking without notes.

Since she had spent the summer helping Bell get started in his congregation, Suzanne knew many of the women from his church. Some kindly reminded her of their names and introduced her to others as "our pastor's wife."

After lunch while Suzanne was visiting with some she knew, she noticed a woman standing nearby waiting to talk with her. She had on a beautifully designed white suit and a lavender blouse. Finally there was a break. "I'm Saralou Lester. My sister-in-law Tess is the pianist at your church."

Suzanne was surprised. Tess hadn't mentioned her brother. Or maybe she had when she told her about all the pictures on the piano.

"I rarely see Tess," the woman said as she fiddled with her purse trying to get it to stay on her shoulder, "but she sees Leonard every week when she comes to the store to copy your Sunday bulletin."

"Oh, yes, she mentioned that. It's nice of y'all to do that for us."

Suzanne could tell she wanted to say more, but they were interrupted. As the group thinned, Saralou approached her again. "I had a strange phone call, and I'm not sure what to do about it. I didn't tell Tess. Leonard said it would just upset her. It's been hard for Tess, living out there."

Suzanne listened intently, turning her back on the rest of the room as they sat down.

Saralou's lip trembled and she looked around the room while she talked, avoiding eye contact, "You know, don't you? No, maybe you don't. Leonard and Tess's family were the closest thing to aristocracy Salina has ever known. Their father was extremely influential in Kansas back in the 30's. He was a wealthy businessman and a philanthropist." Her porcelain face reddened. "You know, Lester High School, Lester Grain Company. I never knew him, but they say he became a close friend and advisor to Franklin Roosevelt. Tess and Leonard didn't . . . well, they didn't admire their father and had no interest in following in his footsteps."

"Ah," Suzanne said. "I didn't know."

"Well, when Tess married Grady and moved out there, her parents disowned her. They told her he was beneath her, and she'd be miserable as a farm wife. Then Mr. and Mrs. Lester died together in an accident before any of our children or Tess's, were born. Grandchildren might have healed the rift. But Tess was as stubborn as they were, so maybe not. Leonard," she smiled and her eyes brightened, "Leonard is a gentle man.

"Anyway, the reason I'm telling you all this is because I got a phone call and I think you should know about it, but you need to understand the resentment other people out there have of Tess. She had such a different upbringing, so many privileges."

Suzanne nodded, "I had no idea."

"You wouldn't. Tess would certainly never tell you. But this phone call—it sounded like a little girl. It was hard to hear her. She said, 'Tess broke her arm and can't play for church tomorrow. What will we do?'

"I was shocked, thinking why didn't Tess call us, and is this person asking me to come out and play the piano? I'm really not good enough. Then when I asked her name, she hung up."

"Do you have any idea who it was?"

"No, I realized later the person had disguised her voice; but I don't know the members well enough to guess who."

"And had Tess hurt her arm?"

"No, I told Leonard and he called but didn't tell her why. Nothing was wrong. I don't know why someone would do that. It's such a strange thing to say."

Suzanne nodded. "Have you ever had any other unusual phone calls?"

"No," she hesitated. "I don't think so. But Leonard said Tess had received some hurtful notes. I don't know why anyone would do that to her. She's had so much pain in her life."

CHAPTER 10

The Family

*C*louds hung low and rain drops drummed on the windshield as Suzanne drove to church on Sunday. It had rained all night, and she feared drowning out the car every time she splashed into the deep, ragged holes in the blacktop. She'd read in *The Salina Journal* that there was a spring under Magnolia Drive that kept destroying the pavement. It had been repaired two years previously and a new attempt was up for bids.

Even with the weather worries, Suzanne was brighter this morning because Peter and Julie both had decided they wanted to go to church with her. She had assumed they would stay at Bell's church. It was more like what they were used to than Harvest. The larger church had a youth group and Sunday School, and some of their classmates were there. But Julie said they weren't friendly, and Peter echoed her. "I don't think they're used to new people."

Suzanne had missed having them with her. The family had always worshiped where she was pastor since Bell had worked for a community organization.

Again she felt resentment rise. She and the children had given up a comfortable, happy life to make this move. But she told herself it was only fair to support Bell now since he had followed her the last time. And it's wasn't as though he had planned it this way. Bell's agency funding had dropped and he was replaced with someone with an MBA who could, they assumed, solve their financial problems.

Peter and Julie sounded like their much younger selves. Every time they saw a hawk, they called out, "Hawk, awk, awk." Suzanne had yet to see one because she was concentrating on pot holes.

"Slow down, Mom," Peter said. "See up on that fence. When it flies you'll see its red tail."

"Yeah, Mom, do you know what they're called?" Julie asked.

She had to admit ignorance, but they insisted she guess. Suzanne watched as the bird flew up to a telephone wire. "Hmmm," she said, "could it be Prairie Hawk?" Her mind was on other things. She didn't want to play. Then it popped in, "Is it Red-Tailed Hawk?" They cheered her and continued counting, crying out "Awk, awk."

Having Peter and Julie there gave her more energy for preaching. She looked forward to telling one particular story. A father punished his son for lying by making him go to bed without the comfort of books or television, without any distractions, just he and God together in the dark. But then the father couldn't sleep. He took his pillow and blanket and joined his son in the darkness, staying close by and living through the consequences with him.

As they neared the church, the rain let up. One beam of sunshine cut a hole through the clouds, and calmness came over her. She had some hope that Monday's meeting with Dr. Talley at the Presbytery office and then time with Bell's clergy group would give her more clues as to how to relate to this congregation. *They may, like Bell, advise me to stop wasting time on it.*

After church, they stood on the sidewalk out front visiting. Peter talked animatedly with Bertha about how many hawks they had seen, and Julie asked Eva what animals people had.

As people left to get in their cars, Mack called to Peter and Julie, "Don't forget. You come meet my animals and ride a tractor."

Eva looked pleased when George called out to them, "When we get ready to drill wheat, you come ride with me" and to Suzanne, "Them kids never been on a tractor. Bring them out to my place."

Suzanne was honest enough to note a twinge of jealousy. The children had connected.

* * *

They met Bell at the Apple Restaurant in Salina. From a booth by the front window, they watched as the rain began again, pouring down and flooding the shopping center parking lot.

Chicken fried steak was the Sunday special so they all tried it. It was a piece of round steak breaded and fried like chicken, then smothered with thick white gravy. Real mashed potatoes were also covered with gravy, and green beans gave the plate some color. It sat heavy in Suzanne's stomach which was still tight from what she called "church nerves."

Julie snuggled close and leaned her head against Suzanne's shoulder. This kind of affection wouldn't be happening much longer. She was growing up. Lately she'd begun developing her own identity. Her blond hair no longer hung long and straight like her mother's. It was now short and curly. And her clothes for school consisted of jeans and cause-supporting tee shirts.

Peter and Julie told their dad about church with great animation. Peter told the story practically word for word about the compassionate father sleeping in the darkness with his son but then added his own commentary. "Dad, isn't that a great way to talk about Jesus? Caring so much he doesn't make you go through it alone. I mean through the results of doing wrong things. It's not about punishing you to make you feel bad, but like that father staying with you when—." He searched for words.

Julie said, "When you have to learn something."

His dad agreed and Suzanne was gratified to know that her words had touched them.

"When can we go to work with you?" Julie asked. "We want to go visit that man. The one who said we could meet his animals."

"That was Mack," Suzanne told them, surprised that the man they wanted to visit was the elder who wouldn't look at her in the elders meeting and had again yawned all the way through church.

"Don't you have a school day off soon?" Suzanne asked.

"There's a Monday when the teachers are doing something," Peter said.

She watched Bell closely. He didn't seem to be disappointed that they enjoyed the Harvest church so much. "I'd like to ride a tractor, too," he said. "And I want to find out what drilling wheat is all about."

"Okay," Suzanne said. "I'll check the date and see if we can all stop by that day. Also, there's a special dinner the first Wednesday in December. I've had calls at the office from people in Salina who wanted to be sure they had the date right. It must be good if people look forward to it every year."

"What kind of dinner is it?" Julie wanted to know as she pushed potatoes around on her plate.

"Chicken noodle," Suzanne replied. "But it's not soup. From what I've heard, it's much more than that. They talked about making noodles from scratch. Anyway, there will be homemade pies."

Bell's eyebrows arched up. "I'm in," he said and the children nodded.

Only later did Suzanne realize that she was committing to future events in Harvest before she decided whether to stay.

CHAPTER 11

Dr. Talley

When Suzanne went out for the morning paper she found heavy gray clouds suffocating Salina. The headlines warned of flooded roads but predicted no tornado activity.

"It doesn't seem like enough rain for flooding," she said handing Bell the paper.

"When it's flat, it doesn't take much water. No place for it to go."

"Aha," Suzanne said, "Kansas reveals something new every day."

Bell looked up from the newspaper. "Especially for you, starting all over learning new ways to 'do church.'" He slammed the paper down on the table. "It doesn't make sense when there's so much you already know but can't use out there."

She grinned at him. "God moves in mysterious ways."

"Humph, maybe it's not God's doing."

* * *

Suzanne pulled up to the strip of stores on South Ohio Street where a white sign with blue letters pointed out The Presbytery of Northern Kansas. Every other presbytery office she had known was housed in a large church, usually an ancient gothic one with more room than they could use. She remembered formal rooms with high ceilings and antique furniture.

Inside the low-ceilinged, gray building a receptionist, behind a glass window, took her name, turned toward the hall and shouted, "Dr. Talley, she's here."

Dr. James Talley – nobody called him "Jim" – stood about a foot taller than Suzanne. He draped an arm around her shoulders and moved her down the hall to his office, talking the whole time. She tried to stand tall, resenting the arm that made her feel short and childlike even though she had on her tallest heels and a black power suit.

He talked nonstop. "Mother said to me just this morning that we've got to get the new clergy together at our house soon. There's so much going on though I don't know when."

She just wanted to talk about the church, but she'd learned long ago that some small talk is necessary. "So," she jumped in, "your mother lives with you?"

He looked confused then snorted as he motioned her to the chair beside his desk. He settled into his high backed chair, hands behind his head, and swung around to face her, legs spread wide. "No, that's Charlotte I'm talking about."

Suzanne bit her lip. *So much for small talk*. He didn't look old enough to get away with calling his wife "mother". About mid-fifties, not bad-looking, clean cut and nearly bald, he wore a sport shirt with a bolo tie and pants that were too short. "Floodies," Peter called them.

"So, you've come here from Ohio," he said. "I was in Columbus in 1961 for General Assembly. A good friend of mine was elected Moderator. Yeah, we went way back. He wanted me to be his Vice Moderator, but I was in between churches and it didn't work out."

This wasn't just small talk. She'd seen it before. *Feminists probably have a word for this besides name dropping.* Finally, Suzanne had an opportunity to describe the reserved welcome she had received and her attempts to understand why that was. "Also they report peculiar activity in the building and strange phone calls. Have you heard any of this before?"

"No," he said and stretched his arms overhead. "I suspect they're still trying to figure you out. We had a phone call asking if you were a real pastor. I think the word 'interim' was confusing to them."

"Who called?" she asked.

"I don't know. I try to keep out of church squabbles, and I advise you to do the same. Provide worship services, visit them in the hospital, and don't even listen to this kind of thing."

"I'm certainly not going to get in between two sides in a disagreement, but I'm concerned about trying to connect with them. Can you shed any light on why some parishioners might be cold, or even hostile toward me?"

"Well," he said, looking up at his bookshelves, "these little churches have long histories. Don't respond to their complaints. Just keep them happy. Churches like this—well, all we can hope to do is maintain them until they die out. That time may have come for Harvest. But, you know," he said leaning forward, "their mission-giving per capita is one of the most generous in the Presbytery. Usually, a church that small can only manage to keep themselves alive."

* * *

Suzanne went home and sat at the kitchen table, staring out the window at the rain. She'd have been better off not consulting him. There was no way she could be a pastor to them and ignore what was going on. But if she didn't take his advice, what would happen if she needed his support later? *Maybe I didn't explain it very well.*

CHAPTER 12

The Clergy Group

*W*hen Suzanne walked into Bell's office, the men stopped ringing the bells in his collection and turned to welcome her.

Bell introduced her. "Suzanne, meet Garry, he's American Lutheran, recently ordained and all his parishioners are trying to match him up with the single women in town."

"No doubt, they are," Suzanne said. "I bet they love feeding you, too."

"Sure enough," he said blushing all the way through his red hair and freckles. He pulled a bag of blueberry muffins out of his denim backpack. "My secretary made these. I thought you guys could help me save the old waistline."

The United Methodist pastor had his eyes on the muffins until Bell turned to him. "Suzanne, Charlie is the pastor of the Methodist church one block west of here." Charlie gave her a two-handed shake and bobbed up and down. He looked like a happy snowman: round head, rosy cheeks, and the rest of him one large snowball. She liked him immediately.

Suzanne's breath stopped for a moment when she met Frank, the Roman Catholic priest. He looked at her intensely with his big brown eyes. "Welcome,

Suzanne." That was all he said, but the way he said it made her feel she had entered into a dialogue.

The fourth was Ronald from the Episcopal Church. He said the right words but his eyes had a look she'd seen before, that closed off, inward focusing that she'd seen before in introspective or depressed people.

They sat at the round table, and Bell poured coffee. Suzanne found it easier to converse seated when the difference in their heights wasn't so obvious.

She picked small bites off her muffin while the men ate less delicately their second and third ones. Father Frank opened the meeting with a short prayer asking God's presence with them. Then he turned to her. "We've all met together a few times so we're somewhat familiar with each other's churches. Tell us about yours."

Suzanne described how different Harvest was from what she had always known as church: the lack of music, committees and organization, the standoffishness except when she visited in their homes. She told them about the women's meeting and her visits. "They say peculiar things are going on." She described the communion cloth incident, the record book, hurtful notes and mysterious phone calls. "One member said they get anonymous calls every time they do more at the church, so he wants to do less. There are only 25 to 30 people there on Sunday mornings. It doesn't make sense to me that such a small group of people who have known each other for years can't figure out who is causing trouble."

They looked at her intently as she talked and nodded at appropriate moments so she went on. "A woman who lives here in Salina told me about a phone call she received saying her sister-in-law Tess, who is our pianist, had broken her arm. There was no truth in it. Tess and her husband are being targeted, and others express anger that they're being treated this way. That's the family who lost their five year old son in a tractor accident years ago. I don't think they've ever recovered from it.

"I've never served a church this small and I don't know Kansas or the farming culture. Do you have any suggestions about how to proceed?" She took a deep breath and looked to each one, hoping to find both some understanding and some wisdom.

Charlie spoke first. "Have you asked your personnel committee about this?" He brushed crumbs off his stomach into his hand and looked around for what to do with them.

She slumped. "They don't have one. There are no committees at all."

"Ohhh," Charlie said, "up a creek without a paddle. Maybe you should tell your District Superintendent, or whatever it is you call them."

"Presbytery Executive," Bell filled in. "She met with him this morning." He turned to Suzanne, "How did it go?"

After she described that meeting and Dr. Talley's advice to ignore the harassment and just keep them happy until they die out, Bell whispered, "Jackass."

Others murmured assent. "That's no way to be a pastor," Garry said. All the faces around her looked down at the table or up at the ceiling.

"Have they tried to trace the phone calls?" Garry asked.

Suzanne explained the phone system out in the county. "Please don't think I'm resisting your suggestions. I do hope you will think this through with me," she said.

He tried again, "I've never been in a church like that, but in seminary we learned that a really small church isn't organized the way a larger one is.

Somebody said they are "organisms not organizations." They operate like a family and their leaders aren't necessarily those holding offices. And they don't make decisions in official meetings, they make them in the parking lot afterward."

Bell said, "It brings me back to Family Systems Theory. I don't know how exactly, but I think some of what we've learned about dysfunctional families will apply to your situation. Maybe they're protecting someone—seems like in a group that small they'd know who it was."

"Good suggestions. I'll pursue them," Suzanne said.

Frank had been silent, but he looked deeply into her eyes and asked her, "What is it like when you serve them the body and blood of Christ?"

She glanced away. His look was disturbingly intense.

"We've only had Communion once since I got there. It was rather stiff and difficult for me to feel like we were a community connected in the receiving of the elements." She paused trying to put into words what she was feeling. "It felt more distancing than connecting. The sacrament for me is an intimate encounter with each other and with God. With them it felt dishonest, rather barren and superficial.

"But maybe it's me. I know I have to adjust to this different style of church. It's unlike anything I've ever known. There's no music except what we can squeak out together from the limited number of hymns the pianist can play. There's no choir, no flowers usually, no stained glass, just a few pews and a pulpit and communion table, all quite plain. I know those things don't make a church a church, but I'm rethinking what is essential for a group to be a real church.

"The most hopeful thing I've seen is how they brightened up when our children went with me yesterday. They actually talked to them and invited them to ride a tractor and see their animals."

Frank was still staring at her. "Do you love them?" he asked.

She stiffened. "I don't know them well enough to love them."

"Do you have to know them to love them?"

This led to a stimulating conversation about kinds of love and depths of love pastors have for their parishioners. Father Frank said, "I don't like all of my parishioners, but I have learned to love them. It is the most profound lesson of my life."

Ronald the Episcopal priest had been quiet through all this, a quiet that seemed to bother no one. But when all were silent, Ronald took a deep breath, leaned forward and clasped his hands on the table. "Suzanne," he said, "you have been called to Harvest Presbyterian Church for a reason. There's a purpose for your being there. What is your prayer about this?"

"It's been a scream for help," she said. "I've been asking why I'm there and what I'm called to do. I've been focused on whether it's a real call from God. The people don't seem to confirm it. Maybe it's a mistake because everything I know about church and how to pastor seems not to apply."

"May I offer a prayer?" Ronald looked around the room. Each one nodded.

"Most gracious God, we seek to be your people. We believe there is purpose in each call we receive, and we believe you offer us guidance. Our sister Suzanne is in a most unusual situation, questioning whether you have called her to this place which does not seem to fit her gifts for ministry nor her experiences of serving you. We ask your blessing upon her. We ask your strength for her. We pray that she may find your will for this moment in her life. Let your love flow through her to your people in Harvest so that your Kingdom, your Realm, might be further realized. Give each of us the wisdom to support her and walk with her and each other."

Suzanne thanked Ronald. His eyes which had seemed to look inward now had light shining from them as he shook her hand then hugged her. There were hugs all around, and she apologized for dominating the conversation. Charlie's eyes twinkled. "I assure you this group knows how to keep that from happening. We meet once a month. I hope you'll come back."

Bell walked them out to the parking lot, and said goodbyes, giving Suzanne a half hug. "Remember, Sweetie, there's a white dove hovering over you all the time."

She drove home with tears in her eyes.

CHAPTER 13

Riding the Tractor

---

*B*ell took Peter and Julie to Mack's farm to see his animals. Suzanne was in bed sick with a cold. "Bell, don't let them on his tractor. It's too dangerous."

They returned bringing their excitement into her quiet room. Sitting on the edge of her bed, Peter said, "It was cool, really cool. He let me drive the tractor a little bit."

Suzanne looked hard at Bell.

"It was safe. We were very careful. Gotta go. Peter and I are playing volleyball at the Y."

"You both need to get haircuts," she said as they escaped out the door.

Julie curled up next to her mother, face turned away from her sneezes. "I got to hold a baby pig. That was my favorite thing."

She got quiet for a few moments. "Mom," she whispered, "is there any way we could go back to Ohio?"

"Why Jules, is something wrong?"

"Everything. We're not happy here like we used to be."

"Hmmm," Suzanne said.

"You and Dad pretend to be happy. Peter doesn't even try."

"What about you?"

"There are some good things. Today was fun. But it's not the same."

"I know, baby, I know. It's not the same. Achoo, achoo, achoo, achoo, sniff. Sweetie, would you get me a cup of tea?"

CHAPTER 14

Eva and George

Suzanne continued to follow her plan of visiting each member of her congregation, first those in the nursing homes, then those confined to their houses. Every one of them needed someone to listen.

"I'm getting worse. I don't know how much time I have left."

"My son doesn't come see me"

"I think the cancer is in my brain."

"Let me tell you about the greatest adventure of my life. One time my daddy bundled us all in the buggy, horse-drawn, don't you know; and we went to Kansas City. It took us a month to get there. We camped along the way. Then we stayed about a month with my aunt and uncle and took a month to get home."

Others were more elusive. Junior was still shy with her. "Aw, I don't need no visit," he said when she asked when he'd be home. "You go on and see somebody else."

Tess's brother Leonard was home sick when she went by his store. Minnie wasn't home even when she said she would be.

Suzanne went by the café in nearby Gypsum a few times for lunch. This was, according to the books on small churches, where she could get to know the culture, but few people came for lunch, no one she knew and no way to connect with those who were deep into conversations.

Occasionally, she'd be invited to visit someone. One Monday morning Eva came into the church while Suzanne was searching for her typewriter. "Hi Eva, my typewriter's missing. Any idea if someone would have borrowed it?" It was a brand new Selectric which eliminated the need for correction fluid. It had a ribbon which typed black on the bottom half and white on the top half. An error had to simply be retyped using the white half. It had been a splurge, but she didn't regret it . . . if it hadn't walked away permanently, that is.

"Lord, no telling. I'll check the basement."

Suzanne searched under every pew and among the choir chairs before heading downstairs. She met Eva coming out of the kitchen with the typewriter in her arms. "It was under the sink. Heaven only knows how these things happen. It got a little wet from a drip under there. I hope it will be okay.

"I came over to see if you would stop by after while," Eva said.

"Sure, I can do that. What's up?"

"Oh, we'd like to just sit and talk a little bit."

* * *

Eva's efficiency as an elder had been quite helpful. The maps she had drawn and the lists of members had given Suzanne some idea of the scope of the little congregation. However, Eva's husband

George was a mystery. He scowled during church and had hardly said two words to her since she'd arrived. As Suzanne tried to avoid the ruts in their driveway, she wondered what kind of reception she'd get.

A muddy tractor sat near the back door. Suzanne parked behind it.

Inside George sat at the white enamel kitchen table eating soup. Suzanne started apologizing, "I'm sorry. I thought if I came this early . . . ."

"No, no, no, it's okay," Eva said. "I planned on you for lunch. George gets up real early so he takes his lunch before most."

"It don't matter," George said, right hand on his coffee cup, left one taking off his Kansas City Royals cap and scratching his head. "I wanted to tell you something anyways. I guess you heard about those damn phone calls."

"I've heard. You get them, too?"

"Yes, goddammit, and I want them to stop."

Eva had her back to them, slicing bread.

Suzanne's insides winced at his language, but she tried to keep her face from showing it. "Do you know who it is?"

"Got my suspicions, and when I can prove it, I'll take care of it for good."

Suzanne took a deep breath. "How would you do that, George?" she asked.

"Haven't decided," he said. "Cut their phone wires or maybe give them a dose of their own medicine."

"If you find out who it is, would you tell me so I can try to find a way to deal with it?"

"Why?" he asked.

"I'd like to give the person a chance to ask forgiveness and—."

He interrupted with a grunt.

"And see if the goodness of the congregation can go on and not be hurt by this annoyance."

Eva turned around. "George, we don't want the church to close."

"Huh," he said, "well, it all depends."

"Will you let me handle it?" Suzanne asked.

"We don't need no outsiders. We take care of things amongst us very well."

"George, we've tried to solve this," Eva said, putting two more bowls of chicken soup and a plate of homemade bread on the table. "It's tearing us apart. Your mother would be so sad."

"My dad gave the land for the church," he said.

"I'll be talking with Eva and the other elders about options of how to proceed. How about you let me know if you get any calls or if anything else peculiar happens. Then we can work together," Suzanne said.

"You want me to call you when I get them calls in the middle of the night?" He grinned then tipped his bowl up to drink the rest of the soup.

She smiled. "The next morning will be fine for me."

He laughed an abrupt, "Hah!" With a belch, a stern look from Eva and a quick, "Scuze me," he was out the door.

The two women took their time finishing lunch. Suzanne hadn't been hungry, but the homemade soup and fresh-from-the-oven bread tasted so good she accepted seconds.

A small bouquet of red and white rosebuds sat in the center of the table in a glass vase. When Suzanne complimented them, Eva looked down at the table and said softly, "George has them delivered once a week."

She paused and then looked at Suzanne, her eyes pleading. "He gets frustrated when people don't do what's right," she said. "He's a hard man just like his father in that way, but otherwise he's like his mother. She was a gentle soul."

CHAPTER 15

Leonard

The next time Suzanne stopped in to see Leonard at his store, he was there and took time to visit with her. In a back room stuffed with furniture and boxes, he led her to a row of recliners where he selected one and leaned back in it with his hands behind his head. Suzanne sat next to him leaning over to hear what he was saying. He repeated what she'd learned from his wife Saralou, that Tess had received harassing phone calls and mean notes. He was slow to start but when he got rolling, he rambled on, eyes half closed, like he was on a psychiatrist's couch.

"I've been concerned about Tess, seems these irritations are getting worse. Our parents also had strange phone calls and they got notes, too. Dad was involved in politics, and they often received them through the years. We learned to ignore them."

He shifted position and turned to look at Suzanne. "There was one time that was especially disturbing. A week before their accident Mother told me she got one of those calls. She could only make out one word, 'die'. I told the police when they investigated their deaths, but they thought it was a random call. I was satisfied it was an accident. But now with all this, I can't help wondering if somehow this harassment Tess is receiving is a holdover from someone who still has a grudge against Dad. But there's no reason someone would want to hurt Tess. She's been through enough hurting."

"Any ideas how I can help?"

"Well, it would be terrific if you could be her friend. She says nobody out there likes her. She's considered an outsider since she grew up in Salina and it doesn't help that she had so many privileges those folks never had. You know, some of the people out there have never been outside the county and only come into town for groceries. I'm sure another thing that doesn't help is that she makes a big deal out of being a descendant of a Revolutionary War General. She never misses a Daughters of the American Revolution meeting, and I'm sure it increases the impression that she's an outlier, dressing up fancy and going to the Salina Country Club.

"Yes, she sure could use a friend. She never had good friends even as a child. She was sullen. I was given too much attention, she was given too little. Mother and Dad wanted me to go into politics. They even said I could become president. I know a lot of parents say that. But they meant it. Elocution lessons, tailored suits by the time I reached high school, lots of advice about how to be popular and become class president, which I did. But I hated it. I just wanted to be alone so I could read.

"Tess would have given anything for a little of that attention. She did whatever she could to get them to notice her. Straight A's didn't get a comment. If she came home with one B, Dad would say, 'What's the matter? No daughter of mine should get anything but A's.' One time he said, 'You're no daughter of mine.' I can still see the shock on her face."

Leonard laughed sharply and sat up. He wrung his hands. "Once when she was quite young she tore the heads off some of her dolls and went screaming to Mother that I had done it."

"That's very sad. Has she ever had a happy time in her life?"

"Oh, yes." His voice softened. He closed his eyes and leaned back. "When she met Grady there was no doubt they were meant for each other. I've never seen her so radiant. Mother and Dad disowned her for marrying a farmer, but I thought at the time it was a good turn of events, her trading in parents who never showed her affection for a man who adored her. It was fun to be around Grady and Tess, lots of laughter. It lasted a while. When their first son was born, they were even happier. He was a special child. You could see intelligence and fire in his eyes even before he could talk.

Then he was killed in a terrible accident. Grady and Tess have never been the same since."

CHAPTER 16

Peter

Suzanne smiled as she watched Peter sitting on the countertop in the kitchen with the phone to his ear. He had curled up with his back to the rest of them. She remembered her own teenage days when she'd try to talk on the phone while the whole family listened so she favored getting an extension for the upstairs, but Bell had made it clear that it wasn't in the budget.

"You go on, Julie, I'll finish this tonight," she said wrapping Peter's plate and putting it in the refrigerator.

He talked with his best friend from Ohio, whispering in low tones, occasionally chuckling.

Bell left to watch the news on television. Suzanne's mind was on automatic thinking about her next sermon while washing dishes and then wiping off the table and counter top.

"Why are you always spying on me?" Peter said when he hung up.

"What?" she said. "Actually, I was trying to finish as quickly and quietly as I could so you could hear."

"Huh."

"Really, Peter. What could you possibly be talking about that you wouldn't want me to hear anyway?"

"You don't understand." He said and stomped upstairs.

Later he returned to the family room where the others were watching <u>Murder She Wrote</u>, but he didn't grab his pillow and flop on the floor as he usually did. He sat in a chair at the dining room table behind them eating his cold dinner. When Suzanne glanced at him during a commercial, his had his leg propped up on the corner of the table examining his ankle.

"What's that on your leg?" she asked.

"Nothing."

She got up and examined it. "Oh my goodness. Bell, come see this. You got a tattoo? Is it real?"

"Leave me alone," he said.

"No, I won't leave you alone. Why on earth would you do that to yourself? Peter, what's wrong with you?"

"Did it hurt?" Julie asked.

"Suzanne," Bell said, "let me deal with this. Come on, Peter. Let's go upstairs and talk."

"His hair is too long, and he's got a tattoo, what's next?"

"An earring," Julie whispered.

"Come on, Peter. Upstairs," his dad said.

* * *

A week later, Suzanne picked Julie and Peter up from school. "Hey there, my babies," she said. Julie grinned getting in front and handing her grade card over with obvious pride. Peter slumped, doubled over into the back seat and hid his head under the hood of his sweatshirt.

Suzanne was trying to ignore his pierced ear, the hair that had grown down over his ears and the tattoo of a wizard on his ankle; but she was deeply concerned.

"You're too easy on him," she told Bell. "Everything is out of control."

CHAPTER 17

Danny Canny

Suzanne poured a cup of coffee from her thermos and stared at the dirty green wall of her office. She was trying to keep her mind on planning Sunday's service; but whatever brain cells were working kept mulling over Peter's behavior. Bell and he had cut her out of the conversation. When she wanted to take back the disciplinary role with Peter, Bell said, "He needs someone to understand him right now. He sure doesn't need hysterics."

"That is a chauvinist pig comment," she said. "I'm not hysterical. You haven't seen hysterical. Somebody has to be his parent. You're not taking this seriously enough. Who's he hanging out with? Have you met his friends? None of the ones I've met has a tattoo. What kind of kid goes out and gets a tattoo at age 12 anyway? That one on his ankle is actually the only tattoo I've ever seen except the one my Uncle John got in the Navy. It's so tacky. Lord, I hope my father doesn't ever see it."

She needed to get her mind back on the sermon for Sunday, but her cold had come back and was hanging on. Her head felt stuffy and her eyes blurred. She read through the scriptures for Sunday again. She hadn't missed a Sunday worship service even through the worst of the cold, but everything was a struggle. One night in a dream she was dragging a sled with a heavy load up a mountain.

Her eyes focused and she realized she was staring at the photo of her family on the desk. Mother and Dad were center front, she looking beautiful and smiling; but no doubt he was ready to fly into a rage if this "nonsense" took too long. Suzanne and her sisters stood behind them laughing at the photographer, who was probably one of their husbands. She felt her stomach tighten. *Heartache, they call it, but it always hurts in my stomach.* The rest of the family would gather in Alabama for Christmas, but Bell and Suzanne would be leading Christmas Eve services in their churches on Thursday evening and then Sunday services. Bell's church thought it important that he be there during the holidays, especially his first Christmas with them. Maybe next year they could leave after Christmas Eve and have substitutes on the Sunday after.

Again she read through the lectionary's suggested readings for Sunday and was uninspired. Sometimes on the first reading, a verse or a chapter would pop up and speak to her. Not this time. She couldn't find anything that spoke to her. She glanced at the filing cabinet where her old sermons were arranged by date and then pulled out her Pastor Record where they were listed by scripture and title. But she put it aside. *Finding one that fits this congregation will take longer than writing a new one.* She sighed deeply. She could ignore the scripture suggested for Sunday and choose something else to preach about. But then she'd have to think. That's the problem, she decided—thinking.

She stood. *I've got to wake up.* She carried her Bible to the aisle between the pews, reading aloud and pacing up and down. A verse from Colossians 1 caught her attention. "Be strong, know the power of God with you so you may endure and be patient and move into joy." *Yes,* she thought, *I need to hear this. I'm working myself sick trying to make something happen here. And they are, too, as they try to live with an irritating situation.* She started to come out of the fog. *This could apply to all of us.*

She sat down and rested her head on the pew in front of her. *I wonder how that happens. I couldn't hear that verse the first few times I read it. It was like one of those paintings that looks flat but then becomes three dimensional if you cross your eyes and stare at it long enough. Now, if only I had a place to start this sermon.*

Maybe I'll begin with the image of the dove flying over our heads, inspiring us and rooting for us. I'll tell them about my struggle with the sermon and how it began to speak to me and I could end with how we might prepare ourselves this holiday season to see more clearly the power of God with us so we may endure and be patient and move into joy."

Back in her office Suzanne turned on the space heater. The wind had picked up and the church was getting chilly. She wrote an outline, a few sentences for a beginning, and a few for the ending. If she were alert on Sunday she could preach without a complete manuscript. Maybe she could finish everything in time to enjoy the family on Saturday.

There was a rustle out in the sanctuary. *A mouse?* She hadn't heard the door open. Another sound. A footstep. Suzanne's heart pounded, her ears opened wide and her mind suddenly cleared.

She jumped up and headed toward the door. She got as far as the piano and spotted a man standing in the center aisle with his back to her. Her heart skipped a beat and she gasped. *Maybe I should keep the door locked when I'm here alone.*

The man slowly turned, more slowly than he needed to, looked at her; and with chin held high said, "Pastor, I am Danny Canny." His voice had none of the Kansas western twang. It sounded almost British or what someone studiously trying to overcome the twang would think was British. Obviously, she was supposed to know who he was, but she hadn't a clue. He was dressed like someone important in his black suit, white shirt, and tie striped with black and silver.

"We've got one of yours about to go," he said.

She was thinking fast, but getting no where.

"Mrs. Robbins," he went on, "is quite sick. Probably have the service on Friday."

Ah, funeral director. Suzanne began to feel her balance again. "I don't recognize the name," she said.

"You probably never met her. She has no family, lives out on Alton's land in an old stone cottage. We can go ahead and plan the service. It'll be brief. There's not much to say about her."

She bristled. *Every soul is worthy of a celebration of the lifetime completed, and "we" will not be planning the service together.*

"I'll go see her and call you later," Suzanne said. "Do you have a card with your phone number on it?" He produced one from his inside pocket without looking, and flourished it like a magician. Yes, indeed, she had just met Danny Canny from the Cosby-Canny Funeral Parlor.

CHAPTER 18

Mrs. Robbins

Suzanne passed Alton and Alberta's plantation house and then using Mr. Canny's directions went one more mile. Crunching gravel gave way to a slippery muddy road. The wheat was so close to the car she could see individual leaves and at a certain angle the parallel lines of the rows came into focus and led all the way to the horizon. A baby blue sky held a few bubbles of clouds and a bright sun, and she could feel her head clearing with the change in the weather.

An open shed covered a row of proud machinery next to the stone house. Suzanne recognized Alberta's red truck and pulled into the deeply rutted mud next to it.

She smelled a wood fire as she knocked on the front door. Alberta opened it quickly. "Alberta, Danny Canny stopped by the church and said Mrs. Robbins was very ill."

"Yes," Alberta whispered, dropping her booming voice. "I don't think she'll last the night. The nurse just left. She's got medicine to keep her comfortable. Come, sit with her while I finish in the kitchen."

Suzanne placed her muddy shoes upside down on a rag rug inside the door. She left her coat on but still shivered. Mrs. Robbins lay in a bed to the left of the door, and Alberta was washing dishes in a tiny kitchen at the left rear. There was only one room except for a closed door at the back. *Probably a bathroom.* There were no windows. The light was dim but rosy from the fireplace which filled the center of the right wall. A round table was as close to the fire as it would go. A dim bulb over the kitchen sink bathed Alberta as though she were on stage in a different world. The walls were bare stone, and rag rugs covered parts of the wood floor. Even with a space heater rattling near the bed and the roaring fire in the fireplace, the room felt cold and damp.

Suzanne pulled up a cane bottomed chair next to Mrs. Robbins' bed. Several quilts covered her, up to her small head which peeked out and looked like a shrunken apple with a few gray wisps of hair sprouting from it. Her breathing was shallow, and occasionally it stopped long enough for Suzanne to wonder if it would begin again. *Yes,* she thought, *this woman is close to breathing her last breath.* Memories flashed through Suzanne's mind, other times when she had kept watch over a soul wavering between this life and the one beyond it. She had come to consider it an honor, to be with those who slid away (or fought their way) back to where they had come from.

She touched her arm and spoke softly to the sleeping woman, "Mrs. Robbins, I am Pastor Suzanne, the new pastor at Harvest. I don't know you and you don't know me, but we are sisters in Christ." *I guess we are,* Suzanne thought, *she's not on the church roll.* She plunged ahead doing the best she could with no knowledge of the woman. "You sleep and be at peace. I'll just sit here and say some psalms and pray."

In hopes that she could hear even though she couldn't respond, Suzanne quoted, from memory, bits and pieces from familiar psalms. "Oh, Lord, you have searched me and known me; you know when I

sit down and when I get up. You know all my ways.
Try me and know my thoughts, search me and know
my ways and lead me in the way everlasting."

I should have brought my King James
Version of the Bible, she thought. If Mrs. Robbins
has memorized scripture she will recognize it better.
She looked around for a Bible but not seeing one,
went on from memory, now trying to use language
the dying woman might be more familiar with.

> The Lord is my shepherd, I shall not want.
> He maketh me to lie down in green pastures.
> He leadeth me beside still waters.
> He restores my soul.
> He leads. . . . leadeth me in the paths of
> righteousness for his name's sake.
> Yea, even though I walk through the valley of
> the shadow of death, I won't be afraid because
> you are with me.
> Your . . . thy rod and thy staff they comfort me.
> You prepare a table before me in the presence
> of my enemies.
> Thou anointest my head with oil, my cup
> runneth over. Surely goodness and mercy will
> follow me all the days of my life and I will dwell
> in the house of the Lord forever.

Alberta motioned her to the table where she
had set two cups of coffee. The fire created a spot of
warmth in the middle of the surrounding stone.
"Here," she said, "this'll take the chill off."

"Thanks, Alberta." Suzanne held the warm
cup with both hands and stuck her feet out toward
the fire. "Would you tell me about Mrs. Robbins? I
didn't find her name on our church rolls, but Danny
Canny was sure she was, as he put it, 'one of ours.'"

"Yes," she said, "Melba never officially joined
the church. Her husband was against joining
anything. But her family has been in the church since
it began. Melba's brother was Grady's father."

"So, Melba is Grady's aunt? Do they know she's dying?"

Alberta hesitated, but instead of her usual tightly closed lips, she went on, "She's his aunt, but she and Grady weren't never close. Melba was hard on Grady's mother." She nodded at the sleeping woman and dropped her voice. "To her Grady's father, her brother, could do no wrong. Their parents were the same. They even blamed Grady's mother when her son Arthur died. Do you know about the accident – Grady's brother?"

Suzanne nodded. "Bertha told me. Was Grady driving the tractor when his brother died?"

"No, his dad was. Grady was just riding along. But the family blamed Grady's mother. Now Grady was driving the tractor when his son ran out and . . . ." She shook her head. "The boy was only five years old."

"Oh, my, yes," Suzanne whispered. They were quiet, sipping their coffee.

Suzanne broke the silence. "So both Grady and his father had tragic accidents that killed their sons." She was trying to take in this reality. "Why would anybody blame Grady's mother?"

"I don't know. It never made any sense. My guess is they just couldn't accept that their dear only son could do anything wrong, said she should have been watching the boy more closely. But he was twelve years old. It was nobody's fault really except maybe the boy's, but people always try to find someone to blame, don't they?"

Twelve years old, she thought. *Same as Peter. The older they get, the more difficult it is to keep them safe.*

Alberta rubbed her eyes and then set her mouth in a straight line.

Suzanne brought the conversation back to Mrs. Robbins, "I need to figure out who will handle the funeral arrangements when her time comes."

"Oh, it won't be Grady," she said firmly. "And there's no other family so I told Danny that Alton and I will take care of it if no one else does. Melba's husband left her penniless when he died. He was a gambler and a drinker. Lost all his family's land and hers, too. She don't have nothing." Suzanne held her breath hoping Alberta would keep talking. "We set her up here. She's all alone in the world so we watch after her. Bertha helps, comes every Monday and brings her fresh laundry, takes the dirty laundry home to wash and brings it back the next week. We all bring her food when we make a big batch of something and when we're canning." She nodded to a shelf above the sink which held pint jars. "But she don't open any of them lest we're here to do it."

Alberta glanced at Mrs. Robbins, and Suzanne turned to see. "She won't last the night," Alberta whispered.

"Let's have a prayer with her, and then talk about the service we'll have when her time comes," Suzanne said.

Standing beside the bed, Suzanne gently laid her hand on the dying woman's shoulder and held the other out for Alberta. She took it without hesitation.

"Loving God, this dear woman has had a difficult life. We know you've been with her all her years, and we celebrate with you what has been good in her life. Now, she's very ill and preparing to be with you. We pray for her and for all who have known her and loved her. She has come from your arms and been welcomed on this earth, and now we know she will return to your arms and be at home. Bless her soul, O Lord. We pray in the name of Christ. Amen."

Alberta wiped a tear. This was certainly a different person from the one who could be so tight-lipped and then turn so loud and bossy. Suzanne tried to recall if she knew how long ago Alberta's parents had died. Maybe that grief was still raw.

Melba Robbins didn't move even the slightest. She looked like a mistreated doll wrapped in blankets, most of her hair pulled out and her eyes half-closed. She breathed in shallow gasps and stopped for longer and longer periods of time. Suzanne searched for her hand under the covers and held it. Her fingernails were purple and her skin a blotchy purple, signs that she was leaving them.

"Is there anyone we should call?" Suzanne asked as they moved back to the table.

"We should let the whole church know. I'll start calling people." Alberta looked at the phone sitting on the table. "But I hate for Bertha to find out that way."

"I can go by there." Suzanne said. "I should go home and check on Peter and Julie. As soon as I have the family settled for the evening, I can come back and spell you. No one should die alone."

Alberta looked up surprised. "Maybe we could both be here when she goes."

"We'll try," Suzanne said. "And I'll get your ideas for the service when I come back."

Suzanne drove to Bertha's wondering at this new and improved Alberta. She was certainly a gentler soul and she seemed glad to have company. *Maybe she's uncomfortable with death.*

CHAPTER 19

Death

*B*ertha wasn't surprised. "Melba's had a rough life," she said motioning Suzanne to the kitchen table. "She and my Aunt Sarah were the same age. People never knew what to make of her. She was always different. She'd talk a blue streak about some little thing that nobody else cared about. Bless her heart, nobody wanted to be around her. Then Millard up and asked her to marry him, out of nowhere to hear folks tell it. He never showed an interest in her before or after they married. They all talked about him marrying her for her money. He drank way too much and then later in life began gambling. Ruined the both of them. Lost all their land. After he died, she became a recluse. Alberta and Alton watch after her. Others of us help out."

"Any scriptures come to mind for celebrating her life?" Suzanne asked.

"Celebrating her life. That's going to be tricky. Can't think what there is to celebrate. But she's lived 90 years. She must have had some God-given purpose. I'll think about it. Sure you won't have some tea?" Suzanne declined and left quickly after explaining her plan to go home now and then come back to sit with Mrs. Robbins.

* * *

At home Suzanne checked in with Peter and
Julie, fixed some sandwiches for them and herself
plus a thermos of coffee to take with her. She also
changed into warm and comfortable sweats and
packed a blanket before making the familiar trip back
to the country.

Broken clouds revealed a pink sky; and
through one break in the covering, streams of light
stretched from near the horizon toward her. She
found herself humming, then smiled when she
realized the tune, "The heavens are telling, the glory
of God." *Such beauty! Why did I think this countryside was
barren? Sky and fields aren't blocked by anything and I can
see as far as I can see.* The sky changed second by
second, the colors darkening, now deep rose and dark
purple. Twilight fell softly on the rows of baby wheat.
All was in place and ready for evening.

* * *

Alberta reported no change in Melba and
took off as soon as Suzanne was in the door. "I'll be
back as soon as I fix Alton's dinner. Help yourself to
the food Eva dropped off."

Suzanne unloaded her blanket and food,
worship books and a legal pad. The warmth of the
fire drew her to the table where she found some
homemade bread. A cast iron pot hung in the
fireplace on a sturdy black arm. Her stomach growled
when she smelled the beef stew.

After a silent prayer and a gentle touch of
blessing on Mrs. Robbins' head, Suzanne ladled some

stew out and sat down to eat. She made notes for the funeral service which was no doubt coming soon. She didn't have much to work with. Melba doted on her brother who was Grady's father. She was not a popular person given as she was to long discourses on minutiae. Her husband's vices left her penniless and dependent on the kindness of her neighbors. There must be more to a life than this. Suzanne's fists clenched. *Surely this woman had some purpose in God's world.*

There was a soft knock at the door. It was too soon for Alberta to be back. Bertha came in quietly, nodded to Suzanne and sat by Mrs. Robbins bed speaking in low murmurs for several minutes before joining Suzanne at the table. She didn't want any soup and bread but did accept coffee. "Melba has had a sad life," she whispered breathing in the steam from her cup." I wonder if we could have done any more for her."

"What more could you have done?" The two women sat in silence. There were no answers.

"I'm still searching for how we might celebrate her life when the time comes," Suzanne said.

"I've been thinking about that. What kind of thing do you usually say?" Bertha asked.

"I try to include what family members and friends tell me they will remember, what they learned from the person and what they saw that was good."

"You say all that in a funeral service?" Bertha asked.

"It comes out different every time. I look for whatever will celebrate the life that was lived and now is completed. I try to imagine what God saw in the person and loved."

"Well, that's going to be difficult," she said slowly. "The first thing I thought of was that she has let us take care of her. It has been a blessing for me to come and visit Melba every Monday and do what I can. It's been good to be needed. That's not much. Alberta may think of something more.

"I know what Tess would say," she went on. "She'd say we'll appreciate the quiet phones. She always thought Melba was our ghost. But, of course, the things that have been misplaced in the church— that couldn't have been her. She hasn't left this house for a long time. 'Agoraphobic,' my Ellen says it's called.

"I never saw her as a mean-spirited person myself. But Grady was really hurt by the way she treated his mother. And Tess was sure Melba was the one who sent Grady's mother nasty notes. These things have been going on for a long, long time."

Bertha poured more coffee. "The scripture that came to mind was 'Judge not that ye be not judged.' And maybe, 'Am I my brother's keeper'. But those are more about us than her. They don't really celebrate her life."

"That's okay," Suzanne said, "it's a start. We could also talk about what was learned from her life."

When Alberta came in, they all gathered beside the bed holding hands. Suzanne placed a hand on Melba's head, Alberta touched her feet, and Bertha was in between them. Each of them said a few words.

"God, we pray that you will give Melba peace," Suzanne said.

Alberta followed, "I hope we never let her down."

And Bertha said, "Let her go gently, Lord."

Back at the table, Suzanne had another bowl of stew and again asked Alberta and Bertha to tell her more about Mrs. Robbins. "Maybe there is something you've learned from her life," Suzanne said.

Bertha answered first. "I think I learned to love somebody I never found very likable," she whispered.

Alberta twisted in her chair, then claimed one position. "I never knowed anyone except her that had nobody. She lost her parents and her husband and had no children. There's Grady and Tess and their children, but she never would claim them. She even lost her family's land. She had nothing and nobody."

In the silence the breathing from the bed sounded different, more labored. And then it stopped.

They went to her. She took a big, rattle of breath, coughed weakly and went on straining to take in air. Suzanne pulled two more chairs up to the bed and they all sat quietly.

"Let's sing something," Suzanne said after a while. "Will you sing 'Amazing Grace' with me? I think that might be comforting to her."

They made an effort and then prayed The Lord's Prayer.

"We're here with you, Melba," said Bertha.

"It's okay, Melba, you can go on. You're gonna be all right," Alberta said.

"Yes," said Bertha, "God will carry you on over the river and into his kingdom. You will meet your mama there and your daddy. You'll be safe and you won't feel any pain any more. It's okay for you to go on when you're ready."

"We're not going to leave you alone," Suzanne said.

They watched her struggling for breath, taking a shallow one and then just when they thought she wouldn't breathe another, she'd gasp and start again. They took turns holding her hand. About twenty minutes later, the next breath didn't come. And she was gone.

Suzanne said a prayer. "She came from your arms into this world and now we offer her back to you, trusting in your mercy and care."

Alberta called Danny to come and sent the others home.

Suzanne drove home slowly in the dark. A full moon and a sky full of stars kept watch over the expanse of sky and land.

CHAPTER 20

The Funeral Service

Suzanne arrived at the church midmorning the day of Melba's service and was surprised to see the parking area already full, the hearse in the middle of the road, and more cars parked across the road at the grain elevator. It was four hours until Melba's service, but the sanctuary doors stood open and she could hear voices inside.

The first person she saw was Grady, setting up chairs. Danny Canny and a couple of other men rolled the casket into place behind the communion table. She waited while they finished, wanting to talk with Grady but Danny Canny cornered her.

She was firm with him about closing the casket before the worship service began and told him that the casket would go in front of the communion table not behind it.

"They're not going to like it," he said.

"We close it to signal that we are switching from a focus on death to a celebration of her life and the resurrection. We put her in front of the communion table so that we form a circle around her. The communion table and baptismal font are in the center with her. She's surrounded by the congregation," she explained and resented having to explain herself. He shrugged and walked away.

Something in him hooks your ego, she told herself. *Take a deep breath and settle down. Focus on why you're here.*

Grady had left while they were talking. She went looking for Tess. Ever since her talk with Leonard, she had made it a point to be friendly toward Tess and listen to what was on her mind at least once a week. Those conversations were always the same: Tess's complaints fought Suzanne's positive outlook on life.

Tess was no where to be found, but in the basement she found ten other women busy cooking and setting tables. Alberta was back in her role as general. "Pastor Suzanne, we need for you to announce that everyone is invited to stay for dinner."

"Sure, I'll do that," she answered helping her with a long white tablecloth. "Do you always serve a meal?"

"Oh, yes," she said. "And Minnie's not feeling well. We'll take her a meal, too."

Preparation continued all the way until 3:30. As the women worked they talked about Melba.

"She always liked my apple crisp so I made some for today."

"I always think of her when we have meat loaf."

"That woman could have lived on meat loaf and apple crisp. But she never liked vegetables. I stopped taking them to her."

Remembered for what she liked to eat, Suzanne thought. *Is that all?*

Then people started coming. They filled every chair and pew. A few late comers, who arrived only half an hour before the service, were seated in folding chairs outside the sanctuary doors and in the choir.

Suzanne, wore a white robe and a white stole that had *Peace* embroidered on the ends of it. She stood to the side while Danny Canny closed the casket. He motioned Suzanne to the head of the casket. She shook her head and went to stand behind the communion table.

The service was simple. Tess arrived only minutes before time to begin, sat down at the piano and played "I Need Thee Every Hour." Grady didn't come.

In her meditation Suzanne motioned to the picture of Jesus with the lambs. "Melba Robbins has been carried by Jesus for some time now. You members of the church and the community have cared for her as Jesus' hands." She read the scripture about bearing one another's burdens. "Melba needed you and you didn't let her down. Had she lived in the middle of a city, if she had no church, I wonder what would have become of her. We hope that somehow she would have connected with good people who would embody Christ's spirit and care for her as people here have."

* * *

A long procession of cars and pick ups drove to Gypsum Hill Cemetery where the people huddled together under a tent. The wind whipped Suzanne's robe one way and then the other. She held on tightly to her Worshipbook.

"Almighty God, we commend Melba Robbins to you, committing to you her care, trusting in your love and mercy and believing in the promise of a resurrection to eternal life. Amen."

* * *

Back at the church the basement was full, the conversations loud and boisterous across the tables which held plates of chicken casserole, green beans, bananas in cherry gelatin and homemade pies.

Suzanne intended to talk with Tess and Grady about his Aunt Melba, but if Grady came back to bring chairs to the basement, she didn't see him. Tess was busy in the kitchen. So Suzanne sat down with her plate at the only empty spot available, with people she didn't know.

They said nice things about the service, and one man said, "Pastor, Old Man Jones told me he was mighty relieved to know he could count on you to do him a good funeral when his time comes."

"Well, he may change his mind. I always tell the truth," she said though she had no idea who Old Man Jones was.

Suzanne was used to this being an important moment for a congregation. They wanted to know if their new pastor could "do a good funeral."

She chatted with them, learning their names and some vague idea of where they lived, but most of the conversation was about people she didn't know and memories of years gone by. She listened, fascinated by the rhythm of their voices and the easy banter back and forth. One man said, "I remember ol' Melba from school days. We called her 'horse.'" He paused. "She was the ugliest girl I ever seen."

Another man chimed in with how sad her life was. "I'm sure old Millard married her for her money and land. It was a grave sin what he done to her, gambling and drinking and leaving her with nothing. But, you know, she never said a word against him. I'll say that for her. She never said a word against him. . . . And you know how she could talk."

* * *

That night after Suzanne told Bell about her day, he said, "You're working too hard. You'd better start taking your day off every week."

"Soon," she said. "I'll be more consistent when I've finished my visits to everyone and get Thanksgiving and the Christmas season planned. After all, I've only been there a few weeks, not nearly enough time to get everything organized."

She dropped into bed tired to the bone, and as she was falling asleep she cautiously congratulated herself on what seemed like a breakthrough.

At five-thirty she was awakened by the phone ringing, but by the time she got to the kitchen, it had stopped. Several minutes later, as she was making coffee, it rang again. And again. And again. Finally, at six-thirty she took the phone off the hook.

CHAPTER 21

Thanksgiving Sunday

*O*n Thanksgiving Sunday Suzanne drove the familiar road to Harvest, her mind wandering. In spite of the difficulties at Harvest, the pace was certainly easier than her church in Columbus where she preached two services and taught Sunday School in between. The sun and wind played over the rows of wheat now showing even in the fields that were planted late. In the back seat the children pointed out clouds which looked like animals lined up for a circus parade. An elephant led the way and behind it other creatures morphed.

In front of the communion table someone had arranged fruits and vegetables interspersed with leaves. The earthy shades of rust, brown and orange added flavor to the room. They sang the old favorites, "Come, Ye Thankful People, Come" and "Now Thank We All Our God;" and Tess played "Count Your Many Blessings" during the offering.

Alberta had alerted her that everyone would be there. "Always a crowd for Harvest Sunday," she said. "Be sure to offer a prayer for the wheat."

As she had predicted, there was a big crowd; however, there was no visiting after the service. The stiffness was back. They were very formal with each other as well as Suzanne.

"Nice sermon, Pastor."

"Was a nice service you gave for Melba, Pastor."

"Weather looks good."

People left quickly except for Tess who walked out with Suzanne. "Have you been getting any phone calls?" she asked.

"Yes," Suzanne said. "Have you?"

"They've been coming heavy," Tess said. "It's always this way after some big happening or after someone does extra work at church."

Suzanne waited for her to mention surprise that they continued after Mrs. Robbins' death, but that was all she said.

* * *

She went home and took a nap on the couch while she and the children waited for Bell. He was bringing Kentucky Fried Chicken home for dinner.

Suzanne and Tess were in a dark, damp cave searching for a way out. They headed toward a light but when they got there it was gone and the cave was completely dark. The phone rang and Suzanne lurched awake knocking over a glass someone had left on the end table. It kept ringing until she got to the kitchen and answered it. No one was there.

Cold and hungry, she cleaned up the water and broken glass then went to the kitchen to fix some tea. The phone rang. No one was there. It kept ringing. She thought about leaving it off the hook, but the next time it rang, someone was there.

"Help me." She could hardly hear it. It was soft and childlike.

"Okay," Suzanne said and waited.

"Help me."

"How can I help you?" She couldn't tell if it was male or female, child or adult.

"Help me." There was a long pause and a click.

And that was all. No more calls came that day. Suzanne prayed a fervent prayer that if it was really someone in need of help, she could find out who it was. Minnie came to mind. She hadn't been at church, and Suzanne assumed she was still sick.

CHAPTER 22

Minnie

*M*onday morning Minnie greeted Suzanne wearing a purple headband and a muumuu splashed with florescent pink and green sunbursts. She stepped out on the porch and took a deep breath like a woman who had been shut up for months. Then she held the door open and motioned Suzanne inside.

The house smelled of incense. And just inside the door, Suzanne noticed a wall covered with framed photos of movie stars, all signed. Beneath them on an antique chest was a glass bowl filled with stones: marbles, crystals, blue, green, red and black rocks. Some were slick, some bumpy. Suzanne wanted to touch them and feel their different textures, but Minnie was moving on into the kitchen.

Pots of herbs stood on the window sill above an ancient white sink rimmed with chrome and surrounded by purple countertops dotted with silver stars.

Minnie poured two cups of coffee, handed one to Suzanne and led the way into the living room. Chairs formed a circle, four were overstuffed and four had straight wooden backs. It looked like a setting for a séance. A low round table sat in the middle of them with a silk scarf draped over part of it as though it had been flung there. Above, hanging low was an ancient looking chandelier holding real candles. They were already lit. Suzanne wondered if others might be coming as they sat down in soft chairs across from each other. "It's comfortable here," she said.

Minnie beamed. "Since Ed died, I can dooo things my waaay. "He always wanted things the way his mother had them in this house."

"How long has he been gone?" Suzanne asked.

"Oh, it's been, let's see, I'm 79. He was eight years older than me. He would have been 87 this year. He died at 72 so it's been fifteen years now. I miss him," she said, "but not much." She grinned mischievously and whispered, "He was reeeally hard to get along with."

Suzanne had never had a widow tell the truth, but she suspected several of being relieved when finally free from controlling spouses or, in one case, a disengaged and extremely boring one.

It soon became clear what was most on Minnie's mind. "Have you been getting phone calls?" she asked.

"Yes, have you?"

"Not lately," she answered, talking slowly but not as drawn out as usual. "But then I've kept a low profile. I thought you might, being as how you had the funeral and all. Whoever is noticeable usually gets them." She paused and looked up at the chandelier. "I want you to know it wasn't me. I'm not the one doing that."

Suzanne nodded.

She went on. "Ed always thought it was me— long time ago when this happened. He ordered me not to do that any more. But it wasn't me bothering people. He was so sure, I started to wonder if I was sleep walking, doing something I didn't remember.

And now I wonder if everybody thinks it's me. I sit in church and look around and wonder which one of these people I've known all this time would be so mean and then I look around and wonder who thinks I would."

"Ah," Suzanne said. "You're probably not the only one. It may be that everyone is sitting in church on Sunday wondering like you, which one of these people is harassing them and if people think they are doing it."

There was a long silence and finally Minnie spoke. "It seems like God has left us. I used to feel God in the church but not so much any more. We just about get back to normal and then something else happens." She looked over Suzanne's shoulder, staring as though seeing some past reality.

They talked about many things. Since she missed the funeral, Minnie hadn't had a chance to lay Mrs. Robbins to rest. She needed to talk about her. She repeated what Suzanne had already heard, that Grady and his aunt Melba were estranged, that she had caused trouble between Grady's parents by blaming Grady's mother for the death of their child and continuing to treat his father as though he could do no wrong.

Suzanne asked, "Why would she blame the boy's mother when the father was driving the tractor?"

Minnie shrugged. "There was no reason on earth, no logical reason. I guess it was grief talking."

Minnie reached around to a table behind her and picked up pictures of her grandchildren who were in their twenties and her impish-looking great grandson, two years old. "They say he looks like me."

When Suzanne walked down the brick steps to her car, she realized Minnie's eyes hadn't wandered like they did in church. And her speech, though still somewhat slow had less of that strange spooky drawl. *I wonder if this was the voice of the person saying, "Help me" on the phone,* Suzanne thought as she drove away. *She could be over medicated. And maybe like she said she's doing things she doesn't remember.*

CHAPTER 23

Clergy Group

*A*t the next clergy meeting, Frank asked for an update from Suzanne. She quickly summarized new developments: The assumption some in the church made that Grady's aunt Melba Robbins had been making the bothersome phone calls; the family estrangement; the visit with Minnie and the possibility of over medication; the calls Suzanne had received from someone saying, "Help me."

"An intriguing mystery," Frank said.

"Yes," Suzanne said, thinking, *You're intriguing. It's amazing how many really good looking men choose to be priests.* Today he had traded in his blacks with the white collar for tight jeans and a Salina High School sweatshirt. She pulled herself back to the issue at hand. "I was curious at first; but now after getting calls myself, I'm feeling the anger and frustration they have felt for a long time. It seems to me that some of them take it in stride while others are deeply hurt. One family in particular seems to be harassed more than others. There must be some reason for that.

"And after visiting with Minnie, I realize that each one is suspecting each other person. Not only that, they're wondering who is suspecting them. This has the potential to destroy all that's good in the

church." She told them about the care they had given
Melba Robbins for many years. "They're different
from any other church I've known, but I see God at
work in that extraordinary kindness and compassion
they had for her even though . . . well, even though
nobody liked her very much."

Ronald the Episcopal priest who usually was
quiet in the group and profound when he spoke,
asked her if her prayer was the same? "Yes," she said.
"I am still asking for clarity about why I was called
there, if indeed it is the call of God. And I am asking
for guidance as to what to do next."

"Have you received answers to those
prayers?" Ronald asked.

Suzanne thought a moment. "Maybe," she
said. "The whole experience of Mrs. Robbins' death
and the celebration of her life helped me see them
more clearly as a church, and then I was able to
articulate how I saw them as Christ's hands on earth.

"Frank, you asked me if I loved them; and
I've been thinking about that a lot. I know it's the
right question. It's different from mine which is more
about how to succeed. But I know yours is the right
question. I'm not sure how to get there, but I'm
thinking that if I can love them, somehow out of that
will come—." She searched for words.

Charlie, the United Methodist minister
nodded his rosy cheeks up and down, and came up
with the words. "The reason you have been brought
together?"

"Yes." She sat back in her chair with a deep
sigh.

"Still," Frank said, "we will pray for guidance
as you continue to sort out these phone calls and
their destructiveness to this Body of Christ."

"Thank you," she said. "It is destructive. Dr.
Talley indicated that putting me there for a year was a
last effort of the Presbytery to see if they could be

viable; however, with this harassment eating them from the inside out, they may not make it much longer. On the other hand, the more I see the more I wonder how these people can exist without the church. It is the center of life for them; I don't know how they can exist without it."

Suzanne insisted they go on to someone else. She was self conscious about taking too much time. Frank said he was in trouble with the Bishop for participating in a Protestant wedding with Charlie, and Charlie was in trouble with a few members of his congregation for conducting the wedding with a Roman Catholic Priest. Ron asked for their collective experience since he was dealing with an unwed mother wanting her baby to be baptized and a congregation who, no doubt, would be shocked.

Bell said, "My secretary has decided I need direction from her. She's started giving me a list of things to do each week. And I'm spittin' mad. Any suggestions about how to deal with her?"

Suzanne was not surprised at this development. Bell liked to fly by the seat of his pants, and she had been concerned about how he could manage a church of 1200 parishioners and a staff of five. There were some thoughtful suggestions for him, but nobody asked if he needed someone to organize him.

Garry the single pastor at the American Lutheran Church asked, "Does anyone have experience with a teenager cutting?"

"Cutting classes?" Bell asked.

"No, I have a teenage girl in my congregation who is cutting on her arms and legs. I've never heard of anybody doing this, and her parents are asking me for help. They won't take her for counseling. The only counselor in town who deals with teenagers is in our congregation. They're afraid word will get around if they go to him."

"I had a roommate in college who cut on his arms," Charlie said. "I tried several times to get him to tell me why, but he wouldn't talk about it."

No one else spoke for a long minute, and he went on, "When I asked a psych prof why someone would do that, he said he didn't know but thought it might be a way of releasing emotions."

"I wonder what kind of emotions couldn't be released another way," Suzanne said. "I've never heard of such a thing."

"I haven't either," Frank said. "I've heard of people whipping themselves. There's a religious sect in New Mexico which even has mock crucifixions. They used to nail the chosen person's hands to a cross, but they had too many deaths and so now they use a rope. I gather it's an honor to be the one on the cross. And I've wondered about that, whether it is a way to release guilt or—I don't know."

"Maybe it's a way to feel the pain they think they should feel or somehow to be one with Christ," Ron said. "But I don't understand that kind of thinking. Do the parents have any idea what's causing the girl to do this?"

"They haven't got a clue. They are totally freaked out, even wondering if she'll have to be institutionalized," Garry said. "I searched the library and found some references in The Journal of Abnormal Psychology and American Journal of Psychotherapy, but they were about mentally retarded and insane people piercing and damaging their bodies. As far as I could tell there was no real understanding of why they did it or how it got started as a cultural tradition like with some African tribes. I don't think this girl is insane. In fact she's quite bright, but when I tried to talk with her, she couldn't or wouldn't tell me why she does it."

"Shall we all seek out information from our contacts and pray without ceasing for this young girl and her parents and pastor?" Ron said.

They agreed to skip December and meet again in January. "Unless someone calls an emergency meeting," Bell said and then laughed sharply.

CHAPTER 24

The Chicken Noodle Supper

The season of Advent began the Sunday after Thanksgiving. Suzanne walked around the sanctuary astonished to see Christmas decorations everywhere. A beautiful banner above the piano showed Mary, Joseph, and the donkey silhouetted on a winding road toward a city in the distance. Green wreaths with red bows hung on either side of the picture of The Great Shepherd and his sheep. Garland draped the choir rail and red candles sat among greenery in the windows. She'd never known a church in which this kind of thing happened spontaneously. Usually she had to contact a committee to decorate for Christmas.

The basement looked festive, too, ready for Wednesday night's Annual Chicken Noodle Supper. Red and green garlands hung low over the sunflower curtains at the windows and a red or green candle in a simple glass star holder sat on each table.

Clouds of chicken steam floated around Eva, Minnie and Tess as they rolled out slabs of dough and cut it into noodles. Others arranged two long tables with slices of pies. Suzanne handed her pecan pies to Alberta who placed them alongside cherry with a lattice crust, golden apple, blueberry, gooseberry, cream, chess, coconut cream, chocolate cream, banana cream.

Tables were set up in the long room end to end and close together. They were covered with long white paper and dotted with salt and pepper shakers which sat beside the candle centerpieces.

By the time the doors opened to the public, the line of people reached all the way to the road. Alberta asked Suzanne to sit with her at the head of the buffet line to collect tickets so she could introduce her to people.

They came steadily for two and a half hours. The names and faces blurred after a while and Suzanne felt her smile turn from honest to tired. That went against her grain. She wanted to be genuine through and through.

When Bell, Julie and Peter came, Alberta announced that Suzanne could go ahead and have her meal now. Suzanne tensed at being told what to do but pushed her pride away. She wanted to sit with her family; and besides that, her stomach was growling.

They picked up their food at the kitchen window. Homemade noodles were ladled on each beige melamine plate then covered with chicken and gravy. Mashed potatoes were spooned on and two tiny bowls placed on the tray, one of applesauce and one of green beans. The aroma from the kitchen was so enveloping, Suzanne felt like she had stuck her head in a vat of chicken broth.

They found a place for four next to an elderly man with a long gray beard and his wife, a plain looking woman with bright blue eyes that matched the dress and bonnet she wore. Conversation was difficult until Bell asked about fishing. He and the man had a long, drawn out talk about where to go and what kind of fish they could catch. Suzanne was relieved to have them fill the void. She was too far from the wife to converse even if the woman hadn't been talking with the people down on her end of the table. The children ate fast, and left quickly promising to stay close around the church.

Suzanne had barely finished her half pieces of pecan pie and chess pie when Alberta quieted the group and announced the quilt drawing. Bertha's granddaughter Mary's ticket won. She beamed and buried her face in the log cabin shapes lovingly stitched by the women.

Suddenly there was a loud bong of the bell overhead. Suzanne had never heard it before now. She excused herself and headed toward the stairs. No one in the kitchen looked alarmed. "The children have found the bell," Alberta said.

"My children, no doubt," Suzanne said.

"It's all right," Eva called to her as she headed up the inside stairs to the sanctuary. "Tell them they can ring it before and after church when they're here if they want to."

Sure enough, there were Peter and Julie examining the rope and looking up in awe at the mighty bell. When they saw her, they looked sheepish.

"We didn't know it would be so loud," Julie said.

"From the reaction in the kitchen, I can safely say that no one was upset. I was concerned that the bell might be rung only in emergencies. In some places it would be a signal for a fire or a death or a birth; but the word from downstairs is that when you're here on Sundays you are welcome to ring the bell before and after the worship service."

"Cool," Peter said. "Awesome."

"You ring it before church. I'll ring it after," Julie whispered.

Half a dozen other children came running and they all wanted to ring the bell. Suzanne lifted the ones too short to reach the rope and helped them pull. She took a turn, too, enjoying the vibrations in the rough rope and the thrill of making that powerful sound.

She invited all the children to come to church. None of them did; but from then on, Peter and Julie never missed a Sunday. When they rang the bell, it seemed to her everyone sat taller. And she felt a shiver of excitement each time the ringing bell announced the gathering of the People of God.

On the way home Peter told her they had explored all of the church. "We found a closet in the back of the church. It leads outside. You should see it. There's lots of stuff there."

* * *

The next day Suzanne found the closet on the side wall behind the last pew. She hadn't noticed it before because it was the same wooden paneling as the sanctuary walls. The door stood only three feet tall, but inside it was normal height. She brushed a cobweb from her hair. Some light came through cracks in the outside wall and around a door taller than the one she had come through. Wooden folding chairs leaned against each other except for one which stood open and held a stack of old hymnals. The floor was dirt. Eva had told her someone reported lights on in the church at night so she looked for signs of someone sleeping there but found none. Dust covered everything. Her shoe prints showed on the floor. The children had obviously opened the door but not gone in. Julie would never have braved the cobwebs.

Suzanne lifted the latch on the outside door and went through it. She saw an old outbuilding, probably a privy, a few yards away. The back side of the church had no windows and the white wood was spotted with gray where the paint had peeled. Beyond the outhouse a field of wheat reached all the way to the blacktop road in the distance, the road to Salina.

Returning to her office she felt foolish about rummaging around looking for clues. Maybe there wasn't anything going on here except some bored children exploring an empty church at night. She would ask the elders to put a lock on the closet door. With that and the one on the front door, everything would probably settle down and they could think about what was really important. Of course, they still had to deal with phone calls; but that could be bored children, too. The voice saying "help me" did sound like a child.

CHAPTER 25

Notes

---

*T*he second week of January on Monday afternoon the temperature reached the mid 60's, and Suzanne felt her spirits rise with the sunshine. As she drove out to Harvest, she thought about Alabama. Such a mild day would have been a tease of spring there, but she knew better than to let herself even dream about a real change in weather yet.

Holiday fervor at home and church had subsided, and Suzanne began to feel more settled, a little less sad about not being with her family at Christmas.

She drove slowly, watching the sunshine and wind playing in the wheat. In Columbus she and Bell used to lead Christmas Eve services together, and the next morning before dawn on Christmas Day, they'd wake the children to drive to Alabama. Peter and Julie didn't know any other pattern.

Christmases in Alabama reenacted those from Suzanne's childhood, lots of laughter and piles of presents, playing games and teasing each other. It was the one day when she could usually count on her dad not spoiling the fun by going into a lengthy complaint about one of his daughters or their mother.

Now with eight grandchildren he was more relaxed. On the other hand her mother's perfectionism seemed to have increased. Even now with eight little ones, she insisted on ironing the white tablecloth and making a fancy centerpiece. And everyone had to "dress for dinner," probably like they did in some movie she'd seen.

Our Christmas was okay, she thought. *Just different.* They had gone to Harvest's candle lighting communion service at 7 PM and to Bell's church for 11 PM Lessons and Carols. Then Christmas morning they opened presents. The rest of the day was lazy. They played games and napped. They ate leftovers from Christmas Eve's turkey dinner. It was quiet, too quiet she thought. But that evening Peter had said, "It's kinda nice being just us."

* * *

After three months, Suzanne had a better sense of her congregation's rhythms. She told her husband, "Bell, I'm going to keep a more definite schedule, especially taking every Saturday off to stay better connected with Peter and Julie."

"I hope you can do that," he said. "I can't promise anything. Every week there are more demands, and some committees prefer to meet on Saturdays."

"I know it's going to be difficult with the kids' busy school schedules and our church meetings; but we all need to make an effort in order to have time for each other."

Finally those pot holes are getting attention, she thought as she detoured around trucks and workmen on Magnolia. She took the back roads and bumped over gravel and lumpy packed dirt.

Cows stared at her as she passed on their little traveled dirt road. *I wonder if they're aware that my car isn't usually part of their scenery?*

At that morning's clergy group, many concerns showed some resolution. Bell reported seeing some breakthrough in working with his secretary. Frank and Charlie said they thought the to-do about them performing a wedding together had blown over.

They continued to puzzle over the issues still unresolved. Ron's congregation was divided about baptizing a child born to a single mother. And despite making some phone calls and searching the books on their shelves, the clergy had nothing to offer concerning the teenage girl who was cutting herself except notations in journals that there was an increase in reports of teenagers doing this and more study was needed. Garry reported that her parents were watching her every move. And Suzanne gladly reported that life at Harvest was calm.

She passed vast fields, now greener, though the wheat wasn't yet waving in the wind like Bertha had told her to watch for. The sky looked like a sand painting, layered with baby blue and pink swaths above a darker salmon shade.

* * *

She unlocked the front door of the church and climbed the steps past the thick rope hanging from the tower. She smiled remembering the joy that ringing the bell had brought to Peter and Julie.

The sanctuary windows directed shafts of light down onto the pews. *This room has begun to be sacred space.* She enjoyed the silence and often sat in a pew to read the scriptures, searching for that week's Word of God.

Her office was chilly. She shivered and reached for the sweater hanging over the back of her chair. An envelope on top of her desk calendar caught her eye. Inside she found four smaller envelopes. Each one had been mailed to a member of the congregation—Alton, Eva, Minnie, and Tess. There was a note from Alberta, "People told me to give these to you."

She opened them, curious yet apprehensive. The block letters in pencil didn't line up straight. *It could be a child's writing. No, each letter is precise. And these aren't the words of a child.* The notes differed, though some sentences were the same in more than one note. There were six separate statements in all.

> *STOP RINGING THE BELL*
> *CHILDREN SHOULD NOT PLAY IN THE CHURCH*
> *TELL THEM TO STAY OUT OF THE STOREROOM*
> *WE DO NOT ALLOW JEANS IN CHURCH*
> *TESS IS RUINING OUR WORSHIP*
> *KEEP AN EYE ON THE TREASURER*

Suzanne first thought of safety for her children. Some of the statements referred to them. She leaned back in her chair and took a long, deep breath. Everyone who had mentioned the ringing of the bell was delighted with it. She wondered if someone living near the church might not appreciate being awakened on Sunday morning; but if they weren't in church on Sundays, they wouldn't know about the other items mentioned.

Looking more closely at the notes, she realized the reason the letters didn't line up evenly with each other was because each one had been traced with a stencil and then the stencil moved to make the next letter. Someone had gone to a great deal of effort.

Moving into the sanctuary, she carried the notes lightly in her open palms like one might carry a snake. She sat down in the very last pew and stared at Jesus and the lambs. Then she concentrated on the backs of the pews in front of her, mentally searching them, thinking about the people who sat there every Sunday. It was hard to imagine who had these strong opinions and yet had gone to so much trouble to remain hidden.

Alberta was certainly opinionated enough to make such judgments, but Alton himself received a note. And anyway Alberta was quite pleased with the children ringing the bell, even echoing Eva's suggestion that they do so on Sundays.

The comment about wearing jeans referred to Peter. He had worn jeans the previous Sunday, but they were clean and neat. Besides she couldn't recall anyone at Harvest who was picky about dressing correctly.

Whoever wrote the notes knew the children had found the storeroom during the Chicken Noodle Supper. The other two statements obviously intended to hurt Tess about her musical ability and Mack about his honesty as treasurer. Again she studied the pews. No one came to mind.

Her eyes stopped at Mack's pew. *Surely no one was seriously wondering about his handling of the offering and the checkbook.* He and Eva both counted the money and signed every check. It was peculiar though that he had brought the treasurer's books to church and showed her how carefully he recorded every expenditure and every deposit. He could have been covering himself. *No, there is no way he'd dip into the offering.*

She didn't like the thoughts that swirled around. For a while, she sat trying to decide whether to call those who had received notes. She wanted to know what each one thought about it, and she probably should reassure the pianist and treasurer. However, Mack hadn't received a note. If she called him, she'd have to reveal what the note said.

Dr. Talley would probably tell me to ignore any anonymous letters. Maybe I should tear them up and throw them away, pretend they never happened.

CHAPTER 26

Decision

Suzanne sat in front of the secretary's desk outside Bell's office fidgeting. She took the notes out of her purse to read again hoping they weren't as disturbing at second glance. The secretary interrupted. "Mrs. Hawkins, you may go in now."

Whoever had been there must have gone out the back door. Bell was at his desk making notes. He rushed to her and put his hands on her shoulders, "Suze, is anything wrong? The kids okay?"

"Yes, yes, they're okay. Some disturbing notes were left on my desk. Would you help me think what to do?"

She sat down while he read silently; then he looked up at her with tilted head and squinty eyes. "Those people need something to think about besides their little drama. Get them involved in helping other people."

"But they do. Not like your big programs here, but for their setting I think they're doing well, helping those in surrounding communities, contributing toward building wells in Africa, supporting the Presbytery missions."

"Well, then just preach and lead worship, take care of the sick. The rest will probably settle down."

"Settle down?" She sat on the edge of her chair. "Whoever it is has no interest in being part of the church. She or he is persistently causing trouble, and there is nothing remotely constructive in those notes."

"Someone wants better music for worship and is concerned about the treasurer," Bell pointed out.

"They're lucky to have any music, and I've seen how carefully Mack handles the money and keeps the books. There's no cause for suspicion. No, this is intentional harassment. That's all it is. And I am furious."

She took a deep breath. "I'm trying hard to be their pastor and build on what is good, but this person keeps clawing away at it. And now—." She sank her voice to a driving whisper. "Now, they're messing with my children."

Bell had to get to a meeting. "Try not to get too angry. This will probably blow over," he said.

"Blow over! I don't think so. This is more than someone wanting attention or being mischievous. This is serious. And I'm going to stop it." Bell kissed her lightly on the cheek and left for a meeting. He might as well have patted her on the head.

She sat in her car in the parking lot with the heat on. *He has always been uncomfortable with anger.* She slapped the steering wheel. *That wasn't helpful at all. If the tables were turned and I were in a church like I'm used to and he had the situation at Harvest, I would be sympathetic— probably.* It was too bad the clergy group wouldn't meet again for a month. They might be more understanding. But then, she had taken more than her share of time in that group. *No, it was good I didn't know about the notes when we met. They have their own difficulties to deal with. Besides, there's only so much anyone outside that community can understand. I'm on my own.*

There was silence in the parking lot, no cars coming or going, no sound except for the wind blowing in the trees and occasionally rocking the car. She started the engine not having decided where she was going. *One thing is for sure, I'm not going to put my children in danger. They'll stay with me when they're at the church. No more wandering around exploring.* As for ringing the bell, it was the elders' responsibility to make decisions about the use of church property. She would ask them at their next meeting.

When she got to the turn to her house, she kept going toward Harvest, still not sure what to do first. If she called each one who received a letter, she'd be entering into the middle of the church family problem. That would put all the responsibility and attention on her when it wasn't a problem between her and the note writer. She told herself what she had learned in conflict management training: "The problem should be kept between those in conflict. The energy should stay with the parties in conflict, and they should use that energy to work out their differences." *Not easy with one party jabbing from a hiding place.* On the other hand, her children were targeted, too, which meant she was a party to the conflict. And she was the pastor, after all, so there was no excuse. Like it or not, she was involved, and valuable time and energy would have to be expended on dealing with this hidden, angry person.

It was hard to imagine that she could figure out who sent the notes when people who knew each other so well couldn't. Or maybe they did know who it was. *Surely they have suspicions.*

* * *

When she arrived at the church and turned the engine off, she couldn't remember driving the last miles. She opened the lock, climbed the familiar stairs and sat in the last pew to think. *If I'm not going to ignore these notes, I should call a meeting to discuss them with the elders. However, they're all really close knit and have been for generations. There are, without a doubt, many land mines. If I start talking with Alton, Eva, Mack and Junior exploring ideas about who is the likely source of all the irritation, the news will spread throughout the community within hours. That would do irreversible harm to anyone suspected, whether guilty or not. Whatever I do, I need to protect what is good in Harvest Church.*

Suzanne stared at the third pew on the right where Alberta and Alton sat. Alton wasn't well enough to be included in any conversations. She remembered how Alberta steered the conversation away from anything that upset him. *To proceed by the book, I should go to all of the elders, I can't leave out Alton.*

Talking with Eva alone was a possibility. She couldn't be the one making phone calls. She and George got too many of them. However, Suzanne knew that she would have to find a way to talk to her without George knowing. If he were around, he'd dominate the conversation as he had any time she visited them. Once he had called Suzanne to come over because there were so many calls that morning. When they tried to talk, they were interrupted again and again with the phone ringing, and he got so angry he went into a long ranting monologue. No, there would be no way to talk if George was around, and even if he wasn't around, Eva might feel obligated to tell him. Then he'd erupt again.

Bertha was the person she'd feel most comfortable with, but she hadn't received a note. *If I talk with her, I'll be spreading knowledge of the notes—unless someone has already told her. Even so,* Suzanne thought, *Bertha would understand my concerns and be the most trustworthy and helpful person I could talk to. She knows the history and all the interwoven relationships. And it can't be her causing the disturbances.*

Suzanne could think of no better next step. It was time to stop hoping bored children were bothering them and all would settle down. *For the church to go on, I have to figure out who is disturbing the peace and put a stop to it, whatever it takes.*

CHAPTER 27

Consultation with Bertha

---

*O*nce they had settled at the table with their cups of tea, Suzanne took a deep breath. "Bertha, I need someone to talk with. There's been another incident, and I need someone I can trust to help think it through. You know the whole story, you know all these people. I'm struggling with what to do that won't cause more harm. We have to deal with this in a way that leaves us healthier. Are you comfortable talking with me confidentially about the church?"

"I understand, Pastor," Bertha said. "Good heavens, what's happened now? You know I'll do whatever I can. We're gradually growing further from each other . . . and from God. And they are such good people. You haven't seen how they help each other and anyone around who needs a hand. Why, it was just last year when Mack broke his ankle, that the church folks and some other neighbors did his chores for a long time. I don't know what he'd have done without the rest of us feeding him and taking care of his crops. But it's not just that, the church is the center of our lives. Without it we'd be. . . ." She searched for words. "Well, our lives wouldn't quite hold together if we stopped meeting every Sunday."

"Yes," Suzanne said. "I'm beginning to see that. At first I thought we could just ignore the phone calls and occasional mischief in the church. It's one way to deal with anonymous actions; it keeps from fueling the fire. But now I don't think so. Several people have received notes, and I'm concerned about the anger that's showing up in them." Suzanne pulled them out of her purse and opened them. "It's hard to know what will happen next. And then, of course, it's eating away at the congregation if people sit in church looking at each other wondering, 'Is it him?' 'Is it her?' and 'Who thinks it's me?' I've already had one person tell me she wondered if everybody thought it was her. There may be others who feel suspected."

Bertha nodded. She sipped her tea and read the notes, then paused holding her cup in midair. "Yes, I'd say this kind of irritation has the potential of eating away the insides of the church. But I just can't think who would be doing this. It has to be someone who's involved, or it may be possible somebody is getting information from one of us regulars." She shook her head. "No, that's not likely." She looked at the notes again. "Everybody around here knows Tess plays the piano and Mack is the treasurer. Good Lord, bless them; they've been doing it for years and we're grateful. In all that time, I've never heard anything said against either one of them. There have been those annoying phone calls occasionally through the years and a few notes, but nothing like this."

"It has to be someone who knew the children were ringing the bell at the Chicken Noodle Supper," Suzanne said.

"I suppose that could have been interesting enough to pass on," Bertha mused, "but nobody would be interested that someone wore jeans to church. The more I think about it, the more confusing it is. I don't know anyone who would do this. But then, I can't think of anyone who would make those phone calls either, and that sure seems to be someone who knows who's been working at the church."

"I wonder if there is any way that could be coincidental—the phone calls to the people who've been active." Suzanne said.

"I don't know. Lord, help me; I just don't know. I am clear on one thing," Bertha said. "We've got to put a stop to it. I am really concerned about the toll it may be taking on Tess and Grady. Someone is being cruel to them, and if I could just figure it out, I'd . . . well, I don't know what I'd do." She put her cup down. "Surely, if we think this through, we can figure out what's going on." She paused. "God, help us."

"Amen to that," Suzanne said. "Now, if . . . . There was something else I was thinking about," she wrinkled her forehead willing the thought to return. "Lost it." She ran her fingers through her hair. Her mind felt tangled. She was relieved to be sharing this struggle, but now that they had decided to pursue the harasser she felt a heavy weight of responsibility to follow through. *I have to accept that this isn't going to resolve itself.*

"Well," Bertha said after a moment, "we should be careful to find out who is behind this in such a way that we can forgive and go on. It has to be someone we know and love, and every one of us needs the church. That's why I don't understand anyone trying to destroy it—if that's what's going on."

"Right," Suzanne sighed. "If we can get this to stop, forgive the person and go on, that would be best."

"I wonder if we have to know who it is. Maybe if it just stopped, we could forgive and forget," Bertha said.

"The downside to that might be that each person could go on wondering who it is and suspecting everyone else." Suzanne said. "That still could rot the church from the inside out."

The thought hung in the air. Bertha was a good one to know when to talk and when to listen. She poured more tea.

The phone rang. It rang once and stopped. Bertha and Suzanne were finishing another cup of tea and trying to come up with a plan. A few minutes later, the phone rang again. After three rings, Bertha got up to answer it, but no one was there.

They continued discussing ways to proceed. The phone rang off and on, but never with anyone there. "Who knew you were coming here?" Bertha asked after getting up the fifth time.

"No one," Suzanne said and wondered out loud, "I suppose somebody could have seen me driving this way; but once here, my car isn't visible from the road."

"There's always the phone," Bertha said. "Someone could have been listening in on my line." She explained that while there was only one party on the church line, there were six homes on hers. The other five were Minnie, Tess and Grady, Mack, Eva and George, Alberta and Alton.

"We used to get a different ring for each party," Bertha said. "You'd know when anyone on your party line got a call. Now it only rings when it's for you and so the only inconvenience is not being able to use the phone if someone else on the line is using it. That and eavesdropping, of course.

"It's easy to get news around," Bertha grinned. "See, you can use the phone system to get the grapevine to work for you. But rumors can start, too, from a tidbit of information and somebody's imagination. I suspect if somebody was listening in,

I'll get a call by the end of the day to see if I'm sick. They'll want to know why I got a visit."

Suzanne sat up straight. She had no idea that her every move had such repercussions. "What will you tell them?"

"I'll say I needed to talk to you about the next Bible Study lesson for the women, and I do. That scripture about Herod killing John the Baptist and putting his head on a platter is gruesome. How can that have anything to do with us?"

The phone rang. No one was there.

CHAPTER 28

The Cafe

The minute Suzanne opened the door at The Café the aroma of yeast rolls, cinnamon and coffee welcomed her. Unlike the times she had come in at noon, the room was nearly full. One long row of tables reached from the front door to the back near the kitchen. Men lined both sides. A few women were at tables on the sides of the room, and one man and woman sat together at a table for two. Men definitely dominated. The room was filled to overflowing with friendly chatter and an occasional burst of laughter.

She joined Bertha at the counter in the back where they helped themselves to coffee from the urn and then claimed a table against the wall.

Suzanne looked around to see if she recognized anyone. A man, at the long table perpendicular to theirs, turned all the way around in his chair to greet Bertha. It took him a few moments to realize who Suzanne was.

"O Pastor, good morning," he said hooking his arm over the back of his chair. Suzanne recognized him from the funeral and one other time in church on a Sunday. He had an unusually full head of wavy white hair. She had intended to remember his name by making some connection with that hair.

Fluffy? No, it was something like that. White? Bushy? Downy? Woolly? Woolly, Will Woolly.

"What brings you out so early?" he went on. "I thought preachers slept late every day but Sunday."

"You must be thinking of men pastors," she tossed back, then paused. "Whole different breed."

Those within ear shot burst into hearty laughter. She was pleased with herself for an acceptable level of banter. At least it had the right rhythm. She'd noticed that what a person said wasn't as important as having the right tone and pace.

Bertha opened her Bible and study book. Rita, the owner, came by with cinnamon rolls. "Fresh made this morning," she said leaving each of them a huge round roll covered with icing.

I'll eat slowly, Suzanne thought, inhaling deeply. *Maybe I'll get full and not eat the whole thing. Must stop eating so much.* Her clothes were getting snug.

"Well, look who's slumming today," Will said to a man who came in and sat across from him. "What're you doing off the farm, Jack?"

Jack answered in what Suzanne had come to recognize as pure Kansas drawl, not like Alabama and Georgia drawls which were softer, yet not total twang like Oklahoma. This was high-pitched and nasal with a swing to it. He talked in verse. Suzanne wondered if it was a certain meter, like iambic pentameter.

> I'm just sitting here waiting for my wife.
> She's gone off somewheres to get her hair done.
> I asked her, "What's this gonna cost me?"
> She said, "Don't you worry 'bout it."
> So I'm just sitting here,
> Trying not to worry 'bout it.

Suzanne didn't recognize the man. After a few complaints about the weather, Will Woolly set him up. "Jack, didn't you use to go to church with us over to Harvest?"

"Yeah, I use to," Jack said.

"Why don't you come, go with us next Sunday?"

"You got a preacher yet?" he asked.

"Yeah, we got a preacher. Good preacher—best sermons I ever heard."

You've only heard one, Suzanne thought.

"No kidding, a preacher with good sermons." Jack said. "So what's he like?"

"He's not."

"Not what?"

"Not a he."

Jack looked confused. Then with timing as good as any comedian, Will turned and said, "Pastor Suzanne, this here's Jack Currie and he's ripe for conversion."

Suzanne slipped out of her chair and shook his hand across the table. "Jack, pleased to meet you. Do they always give you such a hard time?"

He half stood and sat back down looking a little embarrassed; then he rose to the occasion. "These fellows are the biggest liars in this here county. You got you a big challenge here, keeping them in line."

"I know. It's a rough job. Any suggestions?" She sat back in her chair. Bertha was grinning.

"Yeah, they need some hell fire and damnation sermons. Scare 'em. That'll do the trick."

"Well, I'll have to change my style a bit, but it sounds like a worthy task," she said and turned back to Bertha. That was enough time at the men's table, and they needed to get the Bible Study work done.

But Danny Canny, in suit and tie as always, stopped at their table. "Pastor Suzanne, I'd like you to meet Pastor Sam Brown. He preaches for us at the Methodist Church, travels two and a half hours every

Sunday from St. Paul Seminary in Kansas City." He looked like a youngster playing cowboy in his boots, sharply creased jeans, and fringed jacket.

"Nice to meet you, Pastor," he said holding his white hat in front of him.

Suzanne tried to put him at ease with questions about home and school and his church even though she knew the answers to most of them, having been told about this "young student pastor" by Alberta. She offered to do a pulpit exchange with him some time, him preaching at Harvest, her at Gypsum one Sunday. "Give our folks a break from the usual," she said, and he nodded vigorously.

Danny Canny escorted him on toward the door looking back to whisper to Suzanne, "I'll be by to see you soon, we need to talk."

Bertha opened the Bible Study lesson book and was showing it to Suzanne. But Alberta and Eva's husbands, Alton and George came in and sat down at their table. They sat on the edges of their chairs which Suzanne thought was a hopeful sign that they were going to move on.

George leaned in with his newspaper casually blocking his face from the men's table. "Have you found out who sent those notes?" he asked Suzanne.

"No," she said, hoping he wasn't going to talk about this here.

"I just want to tell you that it looks to me like it will never stop. We thought it was old Melba, but now she's gone. And look, it's worse than ever. We knew it was somebody in church because the notes are about things no outsider would know. And the phone calls come to whoever spoke up Sunday morning or whoever's been down to the church working the most. I think those women oughter just stay home and only go on Sundays. Or maybe it's time to close the church. It's just causing trouble."

Alton was so bent over that his nose could have knocked the salt shaker off the table. He turned his head sideways and said in a low whisper, "The women will never agree to close the church. I think they talk about this stuff too much, maybe they like having some excitement."

"Well, I'm sick of it. Somebody needs to give that phone caller a dose of their own medicine so they'd know how it feels." George's angry whisper was bound to attract attention, newspaper or not.

Suzanne took a quick look around. The men at the table were picking on someone else now and no one seemed to be paying any attention to their foursome.

Bertha tried to calm him down and close it off. "George, let's not talk about it in here."

"I don't care." George was unstoppable. He turned red from his neck all the way to the John Deere cap covering his bald head. "I am sick and tired of getting calls all hours. And you can't just let it ring. It will go twelve rings and if you answer it, she'll just hang up and call again."

"Are you sure it's a woman?" Suzanne asked.

"Dammit, men don't have time for such nonsense," he said. "Besides that, Eva's sister in Salina got a call once saying to tell Eva to stop trying to run things. I didn't tell Evie, didn't want to upset her. Her sister don't know no one out here well enough to recognize the voice. She said it might have been disguised but she thought it was a woman or a little kid."

He stood and put one foot on the chair but leaned way down to offer his parting shot, "You know, it will stop for a long time and then just when we think it's over for good, someone will up and get a phone call or a note. And there's no reason for it starting or stopping."   He left and headed for the coffee pot.

Alton said, "I just hate to see the women get so upset. They shouldn't talk about it. We shouldn't talk about it. It don't do no good. If we'd all just ignore it and keep busy at home, it would stop. We don't want the church to close over this."

"Let's talk at next elders' meeting," Suzanne said.

Alton was not interested. "Pastor, you don't know this part of the country. Mark my words. If you stir it up, no good will come of it. Just let it alone."

He had said this before. Suzanne prayed he was wrong. She didn't want to stir it up. She didn't want to have anything bad come from it. But she couldn't stand by and let somebody tear the congregation apart.

Bertha stood up. "My coffee's cold," she said, getting Alton to move. He pushed himself up with his cane and slowly followed her.

Suzanne looked around, but no one seemed to be watching them. This sure wasn't the place to talk about such things. If people outside the church weighed in with their opinions, there would be more pressure on members and more fuel on the fire for this irritating person.

She and Bertha did manage to work on the Bible Study for the next women's meeting. "Let's de-emphasize John the Baptist's head on a platter and focus on how he spoke the truth in spite of the risks."

Bertha's eyes brightened. "Yes, how can we speak truth like he did, to someone who is powerful over us?" she mused. Suzanne had always before related this to political power, but Bertha was on a roll. "You know, the person we're concerned about has the power to destroy us."

"We'd have a hard time speaking truth to someone hidden," Suzanne said.

CHAPTER 29

At Home

*W*hen they left The Café, Suzanne went home without stopping back at the church. She was still worried about her children. *They might be better off at Bell's church. But they are enjoying Harvest, especially ringing the bell every Sunday morning. And I want them there.* Bell didn't seem to care, and she could imagine he didn't know what they were doing on Sunday mornings. In a church that large, he probably had to answer a million questions and check on hundreds of details. At least that had been true for her, before this church.

She baked peanut butter cookies to have ready when Peter and Julie came in from school. She knew it was to comfort herself by offering them what some perfect mother somewhere would.

They came in tired, complaining about how much homework they had. Of course, they were glad to see the cookies. But they took them to their rooms, not living up to the picture in Suzanne's mind.

After dinner Bell went to a meeting and the children settled down for their evening ritual, playing Scrabble. It had become a serious competition. Julie even kept scorecards which she posted on the refrigerator. Suzanne watched for a while, glad they were building good memories. She missed her sisters.

They lived close enough to each other and their parents to have a life together.

She couldn't concentrate on their game and so went to the kitchen. "Thank you, God, for Bertha," she whispered, taking a package of cornbread and some ground beef out of the freezer to thaw for the next day.

Before bed she wrote furiously to get rid of some anger before trying to sleep. She also made note of the idea Bertha had about speaking truth to this hidden person who had power over them. But she was too tired to go anywhere with that and left it for another day.

Of course her dreams didn't let it go that easily. She drove up to Grady and Tess's porch and yelled from the car, "This isn't fair. And I want it to stop." Then she went to Alberta and Alton's, but it wasn't their big house. They were living in Melba's stone cottage. She stood outside and yelled, "I'm not putting up with this any more." In the crowded café she screamed, "This is not the way our church is going to act so just shut up." She woke up feeling great.

She hadn't heard Bell come in after his meeting and he was gone when she got up. He was working long hours. *I was too hard on him for not living my life with me,* she thought. *After all I'm not living his working life with him. And there may be those who criticize me for not being a "proper" pastor's wife. They probably say, "Poor Bell, he has to manage this big church without any help from his wife."*

Suzanne saw the children off to school and decided to stay home all day. She had no appointments. No one was expecting her to be in the office. Besides, she got fewer hang up calls when she was home.

It was a welcome change from her usual routine. She didn't even get dressed, but stayed in her pajamas and robe and moved into what she called her automatic cleaning mode. Without planning, without dread, she dealt with whatever she noticed in front of her. Cereal bowls went into the dishwasher, a load of clothes in the washer, newspapers from the living room to the trash.

She put a pound of ground beef in the slow cooker and added tomato sauce and canned green beans and corn to make her childhood favorite, hamburger soup. Then with a feather duster she moved quickly through the family room, picking up books and socks. She carried these with her adding anything that went upstairs, flicking the feathers here and there, and rearranging dust as she went. She moved right into cleaning bathrooms. It was much less painful if she sneaked up on them.

By noon she was dressed and sitting at the dining room table with a peanut butter and banana sandwich, a glass of milk and her sermon notebook. The aroma of hamburger soup took her back to sitting at the kitchen table with her sisters doing homework while their mother cooked.

A week earlier when she read the scriptures for Sunday, she plugged them into the worship order so she could give it to Tess for typing and copying. But there had been no inspiration from them and she had left the sermon title blank. This time when she read them, the clouds lifted.

"I have told the glad news of deliverance in the great congregation," the Psalmist said. Suzanne let her mind float: *Speaking truth to power, a hidden power, in the congregation, speaking glad news of deliverance.* She took a deep breath and let it out slowly, tension draining from her. Inspiration was in the air.

The phone rang, and Suzanne grabbed it off the wall as though it were a gun. All the anger from the day before quickly shot up from her toes. "Yes," she answered, ready to let it loose on the caller. But someone was there on the other end. It was a normal phone call.

CHAPTER 30

Frances

"**F**rances, oh, Frances, I miss you. We haven't talked in ages. How is your life?"

Why haven't I called Frances to talk about the confusion at my church? Suzanne wondered. *She is the most logical person to talk all this over with even though it might be difficult for her to conceive of a place like Harvest.*

Frances's voice was flat. "I need to talk with you. Chet has been criticized for some of his sermons. Some people called them political. The Administrative Council requested that I preach three times a month and he once. We both objected and reasoned with the Council that he wasn't preaching partisan sermons; he wasn't suggesting how anyone should vote.

"I told them, 'You'll be muzzling the prophetic voice of the preacher if you do this.' However, we eventually agreed to three months of this altered preaching arrangement until things settled down in the congregation. The three months are up now and I thought we had managed a difficult situation the best we could."

"Oh, my, that must have been hard on both of you," Suzanne said.

"It was harder for Chet, of course, and caused some strain between us. No matter how much we

talked it through, Chet still felt betrayed by the
Council; and, in some way he couldn't articulate, he
felt betrayed by me, too. He agreed it was irrational
but the hurt went deep.

"Oh, Frances, this is just the kind of thing we
warned each other about when we first started out as
clergy couples—" Suzanne started.

"There's more," Frances broke in, still in that
flat voice.

Suzanne held her breath.

"He was counseling a young woman who had
been in an emotionally abusive relationship, and—."
Her voice broke and she started sobbing.

"Oh, Frances. Oh, no." It was all Suzanne
could say as Frances sobbed.

When she got control of herself, she went on,
her voice not so flat now, but interrupted by hiccups
every few minutes. "We're both taking a month's
sabbatical . . . getting counseling and catching our
breath.

He . . . he . . . wants a trial . . . separation. I've
started seeing a counselor, but I'm wondering—."

"Do you want to come here?" Suzanne voice
was full of hope. She wanted to hug her and feed her
and give her a safe and peaceful place to process this
shock. And it was always nice to have her around. *She
understands me better than anyone else, and I may understand
her that well, too..*

"Yes, if it's . . . would it be okay with you
guys? Do you want to ask Bell and the kids?"

"Get on a plane. Just let me know when to
meet you. You'll probably want to fly into Wichita
and have me pick you up there. I can make a flight
reservation for you."

"Thank you, thank you. No, I'll do it right
now. And I'll call you back with details."

Suzanne sat down and stared at a vase of
daisies on the table. *Not Frances and Chet. Surely not.*

God, give her strength. And Chet, too. Please give them wisdom and keep them safe.

She called Bell immediately, but the secretary said she'd have him call back. He had someone in his office.

CHAPTER 31

Preparations

*W*hen Bell called back, Suzanne told him
the news; and he was home in ten
minutes, holding her tight. He kissed her with more
passion than she'd seen in months and held onto her
like she was going to disappear.

They were standing that way, up against the
kitchen sink, when the phone rang. Suzanne reached
around Bell and found the phone without breaking
the embrace. It was Frances. Her flight would arrive
the next afternoon in Wichita. "I'm praying for you,"
Suzanne said, one ear against the phone and the other
against Bell's chest. "Be safe. I'll have a nice, warm
quilt for you to cuddle up in when you get here and
hot chocolate and peanut butter cookies." Suzanne
knew what would provide comfort. She herself was
feeling comforted by Bell's arms and the aroma of the
soup.

Bell had tears in his eyes when he finally let
go. "Do you think I should call Chet?" he asked.

"I don't know." Suzanne said handing him
the grocery list. "If you do, you probably shouldn't
mention that Frances is coming here. She might not
have told him. You could wait until tomorrow and
ask her about calling him. Do you suppose we'll never
again have those good times like we used to?"

"It's hard to say," Bell said. "Those were wild and crazy evenings. Didn't they promise a rematch after our last marathon of table tennis?"

"They sure did. It's hard to find good friends like that, ones you can talk with about anything and everything." Suzanne sat down at the table. "I guess I thought that if we talked through all the difficulties of clergy couples ahead of time, we'd avoid being pulled apart. I can't imagine Chet . . . . "

"I know," Bell said. "I know."

Bell left to get groceries and Suzanne made the bed in the guest room. She had put her childhood brass bed in there along with an antique chest and mirror her grandmother had given her and her grandmother's rocking chair. She flipped the sheet out over the bed, then studied pictures of her family and Bell's commingled on the walls. *It's amazing that there are no divorces out of all those people.*

The pictures showed his great grandparents from Pennsylvania and hers from Alabama. She had started out making a family tree of the photographs, but soon realized it would look too lopsided. His family had dwindled to two cousins while hers continued through the generations to be blessed with large families.

She laid out towels and opened the vents to allow some warm air in. It was getting colder outside and the wind was slapping rain against the window. Kansas wind never seemed to stop its constant and intense rush, rush, rush around the windows. It kept Suzanne a little uptight.

By evening the children had their homework finished. Full of soup, cornbread and peanut butter cookies, the four sat by the fire in the family room watching The Cosby Show. Bell was stretched out in his favorite recliner, and Peter hugged a pillow on the floor, while Suzanne and Julie propped each other up on the couch and shared an afghan. *This is cozy,*

Suzanne thought. *It's a rare moment when we're all four at home and in the same room.* Outside the wind blew at a higher pitch and sleet pinged insistently. By the time they went to bed, snow was blowing over the streets.

CHAPTER 32

Frances Arrives

Suzanne jumped out of bed early Thursday morning and checked the weather. So far it looked like she could get to the airport and back provided the plane wasn't late. The two inches of snow on the ground was no problem; however, several inches more was predicted by evening.

"I'll go to the church, finish getting ready for Sunday and drive from there to Wichita," she told Bell.

"Don't you want me to go with you? Those roads could get bad."

"The toll road is kept clear, and it will only take me an hour and a half to get to the airport. I'll be fine."

* * *

The sermon came fully formed: *Speak truth to power; God will deliver the faithful from destruction; speak that truth in the congregation.* It took only two hours to write and edit. Her mind must have been processing the thoughts ever since her talk with Bertha. She'd like to have gone over it with her before preaching, but there was no time. She knew it was risky, but she was determined. She'd ask people to speak up and say what was true instead of remaining so secretive about what was going on. *The truth will set us free. I hope.*

* * *

Frances emerged with a big smile on her face. She didn't look like a woman who had been blown to pieces by her husband's infidelity. Nearly six feet tall, she looked stunning in a long white leather coat and red boots. *The people on the plane would never guess she was a pastor. They might sooner think she was a New York model with that pale smooth skin and her black hair in a sleek Sassoon cut.*

Suzanne had thrown on jeans and her Ohio State sweatshirt and twisted her hair into a knot in order to get to the office as early as possible. *I look like the country cousin.*

Frances gave her a big hug, and with smiles and laughter they began talking and didn't stop all the way home. Frances didn't talk about Chet but kept up a lively account of the woman she sat next to on the plane. "She's writing a book about forgiving an unfaithful spouse. Can you believe that? She had a lot to say about how it's possible."

When they entered Suzanne's neighborhood of winding streets and oak trees, Frances teased her. "Fantastic, I didn't know you'd have trees in Kansas." And when Suzanne showed her the house, she was exuberant about its long family room with the dining room on one end and a stone fireplace at the other. Then she saw the living room had another fireplace. "It's downright sinful and I intend to enjoy both of them. You've decorated this place beautifully, Suzanne. It is so you: comfortable, colorful, and uncluttered."

Suzanne laughed. "Hmm, did you just say I'm comfortable, colorful, and uncluttered?"

She carried Frances's suitcase upstairs and showed her the guest room. "Is it okay to sit in Grandmother's rocker?" Frances asked.

"Oh, yes," Suzanne assured her. "It'll hold together. I know you're remembering how the arms used to come off. I had it fixed. And you'll love this," she said opening another door. "When this part of the house was added on, they put a guest bathroom in. You don't have to share."

"Great. Where are those babes of yours? I brought them something."

They were in Julie's room, their heads bent over the radio, listening to the station which gave school closings. But they abandoned their vigil to greet Frances with hugs. "Aunt Frances, Aunt Frances, did you bring Barney?" They had already been told Chet wasn't coming, but they had lots of questions about their dog Barney. Frances and Chet had no children. Barney was their baby, a sweet cocker spaniel who offered unconditional love to anyone and everyone.

Frances insisted they all gather in the dining room to open the gift she'd brought. Bell appeared as she placed the book-sized box on the table, and Peter and Julie tore into the wrapping paper.

"Wow, Super Mario Brothers, thanks," Peter said pulling the game cartridge out of the box and rushing with Julie to the television.

"Thank you, Frances. We'll enjoy that. I haven't taken time to really get into video games," Suzanne said. "I played Ms Pac Man a few times, but that's all."

"Do you have a computer yet?" Frances asked Bell.

"No," he said. "My elders are currently arguing about computerizing the church records.

Some say it's a time saver, others say it will waste time. The treasurer says she'll keep records by pencil in her ledger even if she has to put them on a computer, too. She doesn't trust them to be there when she turns it back on."

"I've had that fear myself," Frances said, "but we have a computer person at church who has talked the Council into totally converting our financial records and directory.

"One woman I know has been using a computer at work so long, she's already updating with a new one. Can you believe that—she's on her second computer. She gave me her old one and a printer. I'm learning how to write sermons on it. It's easy to erase and you can even move a section of your work to another place. I did write one sermon and lost the whole thing. Nevertheless, I'm going to keep trying."

Suzanne built a fire in the family room and left the four of them playing their new game while she tended to dinner. She put frozen lasagna in the oven and was taking lettuce out of the refrigerator when the phone rang.

"Ellen's little girl Mary had a bad accident. Get to the emergency room. Quick."

The connection sounded crackly, and the person hung up quickly.

Suzanne caught a quick breath. *Oh, no, Bertha's granddaughter.* "Ya'll, I have to go to the hospital. I put lasagna in the oven. Check on it in an hour if I'm not back. Frances, sorry to leave so soon."

Bell said, "The roads are a little slick, but you should be all right if you take it slow and keep to the main streets."

She had no trouble managing the two miles to the hospital. At the ER Suzanne breathlessly asked at the desk for Mary Barnard.

"I don't show anyone here by that name," the volunteer said.

"Could there be an ambulance out getting her? I got the call only a few minutes ago," Suzanne said.

No, they had nothing.

Ellen and Mary lived close to the hospital, but Suzanne called instead of plowing through the side streets to get there. "Ellen?" She was surprised to get an answer. "Ellen, this is Pastor Suzanne. Is Mary okay?"

"Yes, she's right here."

"Good, oh good. I got a call that she was taken to the Emergency Room. That's where I am."

"Oh, Pastor, there's nothing wrong here. Could it be someone else?"

Suzanne thought hard. "The caller said, 'Ellen's little girl Mary's had a bad accident. Get to the emergency room.' Do you suppose—?"

"The phone caller?" Ellen said. "Mother told me about that, but this is more than some irritating phone calls."

"I hate to think it, but that is the most logical explanation. Let's not talk about this to anyone, although you probably will want to call your mother and tell her everything is okay in case she gets a similar call. We sure don't want her driving in this weather. I'm considering several steps to get this kind of thing stopped, Ellen. We can't let this go on. And, I'm so glad Mary's okay."

On the way home, Suzanne passed three cars which had slid off the road. She had to hold on tightly to the steering wheel. The wind pushed the car and drove the snow hard across the road obscuring lane markings. Drifts were growing. She plowed through one to get into her driveway.

Inside, the game was on but no one was in sight. There were no sounds from upstairs. She warmed her hands at the fireplace. *Someone got me to go out in this snow. That's more than a plea for attention.* Her teeth clenched.

Frances came down the stairs her eyes blinking as though she'd been sleeping, or maybe crying. Now that sophisticated model at the airport looked older and thinner, her angular nose and chin no longer softened by fullness in her face, her geometric haircut more severe than sophisticated.

Bell appeared from the basement with a bag of salt. "Did you have any trouble?"

Julie and Peter came running down the stairs. "No school tomorrow! No school tomorrow!" they yelled, barreling into their mother with hugs, and then dancing in circles.

By evening seven inches of snow had fallen in Salina, more out in the county. Alberta called to say there would be no women's meeting Friday and no church on Sunday. Suzanne felt a moment of irritation. The elders had decided without consulting her.

"I've checked on everyone," Alberta said. "They're all okay, staying put with enough food and firewood for the weekend." Suzanne relaxed. *Snow days. They've been more welcome.*

Later, after dinner, Julie and Peter played the new game with their dad while Suzanne and Frances took their coffee into the living room and lit another fire. "Umm, umm," Frances said breathing in the coffee steam, "it doesn't get much better than this: good coffee, peanut butter cookies and a cozy fire." She curled up on the couch facing the jumping flames and Suzanne took the soft chair next to the fire. "What was the hospital emergency?" Frances asked.

Suzanne gave a cursory account of the false alarm and the harassment Harvest Church was enduring. "But I don't want to get started on that," she said folding her feet up under her. "This time is for you. Tell me, do you need to talk or be distracted or what?"

"Well, it was worth the trip to sit here by the fire eating your cookies." Frances laughed taking another one and pulling an afghan over her feet. Then she wrinkled her face up like she always did when thinking hard. "What would I like? Let's see, I think I would like first to hear about your new life and this challenge you have. Then maybe tomorrow, I'd like to talk about all this with you and Bell.

And so Frances leaned back pillowing her head on the arm of the sofa and asked just the right questions to get the story of Harvest Church.

Suzanne gave her an account of the disturbances and then summarized the confusion. "For a long time I felt like nobody liked me. They kept private, closed off. It reminded me of all those times we moved to different Air Force Bases when I was young. Other people knew each other but I felt left out and unwelcome. But back then the only place I felt at home was at the base chapel or a nearby church. I was very shy, but I felt at home there. Not so in this church. It's taken a long time, but I'm beginning to find my way."

"I remember you telling me that during those years you'd escape to the church to avoid your mother's constant push for perfection."

"And my Dad's temper. He flew into rages over even little things. But churches were quiet and peaceful. The people always welcomed me and my little sisters. That's the kind of church family I try to encourage, but it hasn't happened at Harvest, not yet anyway."

"Did you do your organizing thing on them?" Frances asked.

"Well, I tried. It usually works to get agreement on our purpose and then dole out the work. But there has been no way to get a hold on these folks. They don't operate like other churches I've known. Someone told me they are more of an organism than an organization."

"And you can't organize an organism?"

They both laughed. It was a long-standing joke that Suzanne would organize anything or anybody you put in front of her.

Frances began to probe, "Who is the most powerful person in the congregation?"

"Alberta."

"What is the center of their life together?"

"Sunday morning worship."

"Is anyone left out?"

"I don't think so. They seem to have established interwoven patterns a long time ago. But now that I think about it, Minnie is somewhat marginalized."

"Is anyone acting more curious than others about the calls and notes?"

"Not more curious. But George is furious."

"Who is bothered the most?"

"George and Eva, Alton and Alberta, Tess and Grady. Oh, Bertha and Minnie, too."

Not getting very far with those questions, Frances began a different line of thought. "You describe confusion and lies. Those are two indications of evil at work. Remember that seminar we went to, *The Principalities and Powers?*"

Suzanne thought for a while, got up to poke the fire. "I hadn't thought of this as signs of evil, but maybe I should. There certainly is confusion and I guess you could say 'lies' since the person is acting out of a hidden place."

"It's that slippery road toward evil which starts when someone doesn't admit to sinfulness.

"That fits," Suzanne said, "but no one comes to mind right away. Mack is the treasurer—he's a simple man, an open book. I don't see any confusion or lies in him. Alberta and Alton are leaders of the church—there is some pride, maybe some frustration, but no lies or confusion as far as I know. Eva and her husband George—he's angry, 'hopping mad' as he puts it; but I don't see any confusion in him. Bertha—I've only seen loving thoughts, deep faith and protection of the community. Tess and Grady— hard to say, general tension and anxiety, lots of grief, tremendous grief," she said and explained their losses to Frances. "It's hard to imagine what they've gone through. Oh, and there's Minnie. She's quite a character—now, there is confusion surrounding her and she's mischievous, but as far as I can see, she isn't destructive . . . probably. There are others who attend, but no one I can think of who knows everything that's going on. Well, no, there is one more person, Junior. He's the youngest member of the church, twenty-something, and an elder. I haven't been able to break through his reserve even though I've had some success with others. It seems like each one of them is surrounded by a Plexiglas wall, except for Bertha. But, no, I don't see any pattern of lies and confusion except from the person sending those the notes and making the phone calls."

"Could someone be suffering from dementia?" Frances asked.

"That's worth considering," Suzanne said, "especially since no one can figure out who it is. I've also wondered if it's someone drinking a lot or overmedicated. Or, it just occurred to me—since the actions don't fit what we know about any of these people, perhaps someone has a split personality. There have been items lost then appearing in strange places in the church. That could be a sign of a split. But that's so rare it's a long shot.

"It's all especially puzzling since these are good people. They are being the church,. . . I think. It's been difficult for me to see that because it's so different from any other church I've ever known. I've spent some time thinking about that. Not every group that calls itself a church is one."

"You've been there for four months now," Frances said. "What do you think?"

"I'm growing to appreciate them for who they are," Suzanne said, picking up their coffee cups. "And I've been reading Bonhoeffer again, Life Together, and also Hans Kung's book The Church. They have both given me much to think about. Father Frank from our clergy group had two copies of the Kung book and gave me one of them."

"I haven't read that," Frances said. "Save me the trouble. What did he say?"

"Oh, so much. It's sitting there by you. I'll get some more coffee." When she returned Frances was reading her underlines in the book.

"Looks like a whole book about what church is and is not."

Suzanne grinned. "I guess that's why he titled it 'The Church'."

France pretended to throw the book at her. "Okay, smarty, give me a summary in thirty words or less."

"Let's see. The whole book is about defining what church is and does so I was really motivated to read it. I hear him saying that the Kingdom of God or the Realm of God is not out there somewhere, but it's right in the midst of the People of God at worship together—even in my little, insignificant church—and that the front line between God's kingdom and the Realm of evil runs right through the heart of each individual making choices for good or evil. But he still sees congregations connected to each other, a more inclusive body of Christ.

"What spoke to me was the idea that what happens at Harvest matters. Maybe the choices—even in this tiny church—are important in the Realm of God. I think I had fallen into an unexamined assumption that the Kingdom of God is a conglomeration of all churches or all Christians. And I can see now that I had subconsciously assumed that it's only significant to the Kingdom of God what happens in ecumenical groups and the large churches, those with power and influence."

Suzanne became self conscious of her own intensity. "Hey, you didn't come here to work! Let's lighten this up. You know when you ask a preacher about anything, you always get a sermon."

"Don't you know it? Just wait till I get going. But seriously, that sounds really important. I've never looked at church that way, and I'm going to steal that thought for a sermon." She sat up to drink her coffee.

"It's too bad your Sunday worship has been cancelled. I don't get to hear a good sermon very often. Even though I hear Chet preach, it doesn't count since we know what each other is going to say before we say it." She looked down and blinked hard then jerked her head up. "Are there any more cookies to go with this coffee?"

CHAPTER 33

Evil

"*H*e is being such an ass," Frances began. "And I'm not going to stand for it. He should be more mature than this. He knows the dangers of transference and counter transference." Her voice rose. "He knows it's his responsibility to maintain a professional relationship. He knows the power inherent in the role of pastor. He knows it all and has even taught others about ethical boundaries." She slumped over the table with her head in her hands.

Full of pancakes the children had gone outside to enjoy their snow day and sled with neighborhood friends. The three pastors lingered around the breakfast table.

"What was he thinking?" Frances stifled a sob. "We even talked about how vulnerable he would be when he took the ego hit from the Administrative Council. Now, damn it, he thinks he's in love with this little girl and nobody can talk any sense into him. He says he feels young again."

"Who knows about this?" Bell asked. "Congregation? District Superintendent?"

"I don't know," she said. "Surely he hasn't spread the word around First Methodist, but I don't know. He may be so out of touch that he's telling everybody." She started stacking the plates on the table.. "As far as I know, just our counselors, the District Superintendent and . . . her."

As they went on talking, jumping from one thing to another, Bell kept bringing her back to ways this might play out in the congregation. "I'm trying to think if there is any danger to your futures as pastors."

As they explored the practicalities, Suzanne's mind kept going back to Frances's reminder of the characteristics of evil. Even though she couldn't pinpoint a person, the situation at Harvest certainly was confusing and there was hiddenness and destruction. Without knowing who it was, it was hard to imagine getting a confession. And without the person admitting the truth, the sin would continue to grow and become evil.

At a lull she mentioned this. "So, I'm thinking that in my situation if the person bothering the congregation doesn't tell the truth, that sin keeps growing and forming more and more complex problems. Doesn't that apply to your situation, too? Isn't there a need for confession there, also, some acknowledgement of sin?"

"Yes, yes." Frances took a stack of dishes to the kitchen and returned to her chair. "I said to him not too long ago that we were likely the only couple in Columbus who could safely have sex without protection. I assumed he had been as faithful as I have. Of course, even if they haven't um . . . , there are other ways of being unfaithful. He hasn't really approached this whole thing as sin."

"Is the covenant between you broken, or are you wondering if it is?" Suzanne asked.

"I don't know. He just laid it on me one night and left. All he said was, 'My whole life is about to change. I'm in love with Josie.'" Frances began to sob, grabbing tissues from the box Bell had put nearby. He looked near to tears, too.

Soon all three had tissues in hand, and Suzanne suggested that this was a good time to move from the dining room table and build a fire in the family room. She and Frances were still in their pajamas, and she could feel the wind in her bones. It was whipping around the sides of the house and down the chimney. Julie called to say they were inside having hot chocolate at a friend's house and could they stay a while. Suzanne said to her, "Be sweet," and whispered up into the air, "Thank you."

Frances cuddled up in the quilt on the couch, clutching it around her neck, her face above it red. She dabbed at tears which rolled down her cheeks. Bell sat in his recliner and Suzanne leaned back in her big chair and wrapped herself in an afghan. Neither of the others picked up on Suzanne's persistent thought that admitting one had sinned was needed in both Frances's situation and in Harvest's.

At a lull, she brought it up again, "Until Chet sees this as sin, he won't admit that it is wrong and it will go on compounding. Until my harassing church member confesses to doing wrong and turns from it, the destructiveness will eat away at her (or him) and the church."

Bell looked thoughtful. "It could be that Chet sees what he's doing as the right thing, somehow convincing himself that God has led him to this. It's hard for us to see it that way, but he's always been so conscientious that I'm trying to imagine what's going on in his mind."

"Yes," Frances said slowly. "Yes, I'm sure he has somehow determined that this is an exception to the rule. Maybe that's the trap so many clergy are falling into. Otherwise, I don't understand how he can be so blind."

"So," Suzanne went on, thinking as she talked, "it is of the greatest importance in each situation that truth be told about what is going on."

"Yes, but it's awfully hard to see what is true when we're swayed by self interest," Bell said.

CHAPTER 33

Minnie

*M*innie called on Monday morning at six. Bell was snoring, and Suzanne was almost awake. She took the stairs with her eyes closed. "We've got to get another phone line put in."

"Pastor," Minnie said, "my sons are here. Both my sons came to see me, and I can't wait for you to meet them. Come for lunch, twelve noon."

"Oh, Minnie, I have company from Ohio, my best friend Frances is here and . . .," Suzanne started to explain.

"Bring your friend. Oh, and don't worry, the blacktop road has been plowed. We'll see you both at noon. You'll love my sons. Just wait until you meet them."

Frances was game for the adventure. *And,* Suzanne thought, *the distraction.* She had no doubt it would be that and more. Minnie always managed to entertain.

She stood on the porch holding the screen door open waiting for them. Suzanne had never seen her so animated. "Come in, come in," she said.

Later, Suzanne hoped she hadn't stared with her mouth hanging open when Minnie introduced her sons, but that's how she felt. Robert and Richard were identical twins, movie star handsome and over six feet tall. They were both dressed like cowboys though not identically and not looking as cheesy as the young Methodist pastor had at The Café. No, they looked like the real thing to her. Robert looked like a tall Roy Rogers; and Richard was dressed in black like the Lone Ranger, though without a mask. Both were tanned golden and had gray-streaked black hair which could have been used for a Grecian Formula ad. They had Minnie's nose, straight and slightly pointed, perfect if ever God had made one . . . or three. The only thing which marred their perfection was the stubble. It was obvious that neither one had shaved that morning.

Robert shook hands with Suzanne, a two-handed warm welcome. "Pastor, Pastor, we've heard so many good things and couldn't wait to meet you; and so we planned a special trip." He winked and glanced at his mother who was beaming.

They all settled into what Suzanne thought of as Minnie's séance circle. The chatter never stopped as the brothers asked Frances and Suzanne how they got to this part of the country, and Minnie served them each a plate with what she called her boys' favorite sandwich and chips. It was egg salad with melted provolone on a croissant.

Minnie broke in with, "Dooo youuu recognize the chips?"

"Must be Yoders." Robert smiled at her. "Still can't find them anywhere but here. Best chips in the world."

"Mama treats us right," Richard said. "We come back home regularly to remember how we should be treated."

"And to try to convince her to come back to California and teach our wives," Robert said.

It took a while for Suzanne to realize that the boys had grown up in California and visited Harvest regularly when their grandmother was alive. This was her house. Suzanne remembered then that Minnie had said her husband Ed always wanted things done the way his mother did them and insisted on retiring back in Harvest in this house where he had grown up.

"Minnie, where were you brought up?" Suzanne asked.

"Oooo, I was a California girl."

Robert and Richard broke into song as though on cue, "Wish they all could be California girls."

Minnie went right on talking. "We lived in San Diego."

"She was a movie star," Robert said.

"Really?" Frances asked.

"Yes, really," Richard smiled, and Suzanne could see Minnie's impish smile in his.

Minnie laughed and left the room to get more sandwiches. Robert filled them in. "Dad was in the Navy; and once when he was gone, Mama went with her friend Connie Talmadge to a movie shoot. Connie was a big silent movie star. She and her sisters liked to have Mama around so they would suggest her for bit parts every chance they had."

"Dad didn't like it," Richard said.

Minnie walked back in. "And he was furious when he saw you two in a magazine ad. How could he be angry with me? You were too cute to keep to ourselves. We had to share you with the world." She made a flourish with the plate and managed to get it to the table without losing anything.

She sat down tossing her shawl over her shoulder and then noticed they needed more coffee. Suzanne was up quickly. "I'll get it." And Robert joined her in the kitchen.

As she filled the coffee server and he took cream from the refrigerator, Robert asked, "Have you noticed anything unusual with Mom lately?"

"In what way?"

"I got an anonymous note from somebody saying she had Alzheimer's. Have you noticed anything like that?" he asked.

"Sometimes her eyes look unfocused and she's occasionally unsteady on her feet."

"Well, we're concerned about her. The doctor said she's been filling one of her prescriptions too often. He wonders if she's taking too much, that maybe she's confused about whether she's taken it in a day. We're going to set up her pills for a month and then have a nurse come out to check on her and set up the next month."

Suzanne started to ask if his mother had done things she didn't remember but then decided not to alarm him or put ideas in his head.

While Suzanne poured coffee and Robert offered cream and sugar, Richard was going on and on about how his mother favored him and always had. "Huh uh," Robert said. "She always called both of us Robert. I think that says something."

"Yes, that's cause you were always in trouble."

They both started talking and laughing at the same time; and Minnie started talking over them. "I went to the ear doctor—could hear a thing out of my right ear. I had tried to wash it out, but—."

Oh, no, not the ear story!" Richard screamed.

Minnie went right on. "That nurse squirted something in there and all this yellow and green stuff came out. You wouldn't believe how much came out in that sink."

Both boys were laughing and covering their ears. "No, no, no, not the ear story."

"These boys get out of hand sometimes, but the ear story always stops them," Minnie said winking at Suzanne and Frances.

Suzanne started to make a move toward leaving but then Richard asked his mother how

Grady was. From their conversation Suzanne pieced together that they were the same age as Grady; and when they would come from California to see their grandparents in Harvest, they spent time with him.

"Grady's mother and I were dear friends," Minnie said. "We would visit while the boys played together from the time they were all little squirts."

"Is Grady any better?" Robert asked.

"About the same," Minnie said. "But he still has Lassie."

"Remember when he got his first Lassie?" Richard asked. He turned to Suzanne and Frances. "It was the day his little brother was buried. He died in a tractor accident. Twelve years old. We were fourteen. After the funeral service, Robert and I went walking with him. Nobody said a word, we just walked. Grady was a mess. Couldn't stop crying and he didn't care who saw him. We walked out toward the old Hammond place and over the south field into that stand of trees by Skunk Creek. Grady just kept walking; and we stayed right beside him, glad we could do something, be with him, anything. Then this beautiful collie jumped over the creek and walked right up to Grady like she knew him. It was so unbelievable. She came out of nowhere. Grady said she looked just like Lassie on television."

"No, not television," Robert broke in. "Remember they couldn't get much of a signal out here till recently. He had seen the movie. He even wondered if she was the real Lassie, if she had run away and ended up here."

"He never found who the dog belonged to." Richard said. "She was his best pal from then on."

"When that dog died, it was pretty old," Minnie added. "It was right out in front of this house, hit by a car or more likely a truck hauling grain to the elevator in the dark. I found him in the morning. He was dead, his guts spilling out. I tucked them back in best I could, wrapped him in an old blanket, then put him in my pickup and took him on home to Grady. Carried him right into the barn and laid him at Grady's feet. He didn't say anything and I didn't say anything, but at least he didn't find Lassie out in the road. We never mentioned it . . . ever. Now he has Lassie 3 or maybe it's 4."

"He sure loves animals," Richard said.

"Yep, he's the most compassionate person I've ever known," Robert said. "He won't even kill a fly, just waves it over to a door and shoos it outside."

They were all quiet for a moment.

"I'd like to get hold of whoever's sending nasty notes to him and Tess and give them what-for," Minnie said. "It's not fair - they've had enough grief."

CHAPTER 35

The Neighborhood

*I*n the car Suzanne tried to apologize for the length of the visit; but Frances said, "Minnie and her sons take up all of the air in a room, but I'm fascinated. This is a world I've never seen before."

Frances figured out that "Uncle George" was the George whose rants Suzanne had told her about.

"So, Eva's George and Minnie's late husband Ed must have been brothers," Suzanne said.

"Did you notice that when Richard was teasing his mother, his right eyebrow arched up; and when Robert was teasing, his left eyebrow arched?" Frances said.

She wanted to see the church and drive around so Suzanne showed her the sanctuary with the picture of Jesus the Great Shepherd and her office and the basement. They drove by Alton and Alberta's southern mansion. The road had been plowed, but snow covered the fields for as far as they could see. The wheat, having been planted early in their fields, could be seen bravely standing up, dark green in places where the wind had plowed across the field. They passed Tess and Grady's where Lassie sat in the sun on the porch. Suzanne also pointed out Eva and George's farm on the way to Gypsum.

They had coffee at The Café. Nobody else was there. "There is no other place to eat in Gypsum," Suzanne said. "The Café stops serving between 1:30 and 4, but the coffee is on all day. Anyone can stop in dawn to dusk, get a cup, and put some coins in the dish. If you take the last cup, you're expected to make a new pot." She pointed to the instructions taped on the counter. Suzanne described the kind of banter which went on, and they examined the pictures on the wall. "Flood capital of the world," a framed newspaper proclaimed. Beside it was a more recent picture of the levee which surrounded the town.

Then with coats on, hoods up, and gloves in place, they walked down the main street to pick up the church mail at the post office and look in windows: The Grocery, The Bar, The Thrift Store. They stepped carefully through the snow covered sidewalks.

"They tell me there used to be two opera houses here, and over there at the old schoolhouse the boys played basketball every night," Suzanne said. They retraced their steps back to the car which was blessedly warm from sitting in the sun.

On the way home, without planning it, Suzanne turned into Bertha's drive. Someone had scraped most of the snow off and pushed it to the side. "This is Bertha's house. She reminds me of my grandmother. Let's see if she's home."

She was outside feeding the chickens in a small area cleared of snow. Suzanne watched as the two women met, so different in height and build and sophistication. But they had a similar spirit about them.

Bertha was interested in their lunch at Minnie's. "Those boys haven't been to see me yet, but they'll come by. Their chocolate chip cookies are ready for them so I know they won't leave town without seeing me. Such nice boys, they've always been very protective of their mother. Their dad was a Navy man and a little, oh, I guess you'd say 'different,' but then aren't we all?" She laughed her under-the-breath chuckle.

Frances said, "I've never fed chickens. May I?"

Bertha smiled and handed her the pail, then went on about Minnie's sons. "Aren't they handsome? They always have been, but they were smart not to get into show business. When their dad finally accepted that they weren't going to come to Kansas when he retired, he advised them to do something show business people needed. They've made a fortune selling shoes to the rich and famous and those who want to be rich and famous."

"Was their dad away from home a lot with the Navy?" Suzanne asked.

"Yes, quite a bit," Bertha said. "Every time he'd go off on a ship, Minnie would take those babies to try to get them modeling jobs. When Ed found out, he had a fit. He didn't like Minnie's friends, didn't like the California life style, and didn't like her working. He retired early and moved here, but the boys were grown and stayed in California. That's been over twenty years now."

Frances was spreading the chicken feed, imitating Bertha's sweep and talking to them, "Here, chicky, chicky. Come, get some. You guys over there, here's some for you."

Over tea, Bertha asked Frances about herself in a gentle way, and soon she was telling about her church in Columbus. Bertha's kind attention prompted her to say some about her husband and their current difficulty.

Then Frances changed the subject. "It's great fun for me to see where Suzanne lives and works. It looks to me like she's still getting more done in one day than anyone else. I suspect it's by organizing every minute."

"Hmmm, I guess so," Suzanne murmured, used to being teased about her desire to have everything neat and orderly. "Bertha, were Minnie's husband and George brothers?"

"Oh, yes," she said. "George and Ed and my Bob, too. They all grew up in the house where Minnie is now and they worked the land out where Eva and George live. George was the oldest and his father left everything to him, told him to take care of the younger two.

"They worked the farm together for a while, but then . . . well, let's just say we decided to come over here and farm this land my grandparents left me. And Minnie's Ed had no interest in farming. He was set on joining the Navy from an early age. That's how he ended up in California where he met her. You'd have to have a family tree to figure us all out. But don't bother. It's not important. Everybody's related so we don't usually distinguish families among us except for a couple of generations. Most of us come from a few homesteaders; for instance, Alberta and I have the same great grandmother. And then a few people like Tess and Mack have come out here from other towns. Sometimes they're called outliers.

"I'm actually considered an outsider, too, since I was raised in Salina. Doesn't matter that my family has farmed this land for generations. But it's home to me, and now my sweet granddaughter Mary likes it out here. I've been meaning to tell you, she wants to be baptized in our church on Easter." Bertha beamed and they all held their teacups up in a toast.

CHAPTER 36

Speaking the Truth

*O*n Saturday Frances asked if she could stay another week. "I want you to stay forever," Suzanne said. "We love having you here, but is it the best thing for you?"

Frances stared out the kitchen window. "I think so. I have a phone conversation scheduled with my counselor and my District Superintendent Monday morning. I'll tell them staying another week here is better than drinking myself into a stupor." She chuckled. "Let's see, what else could I say? Better than gambling in Vegas?"

"All right, all right," Suzanne said. "Anyway, you know you have to stay until you figure out the Harvest Church mystery, don't you?"

"I've been thinking and praying about that," Frances said. "From what you've told me, I can't imagine a motive. My best hunch is someone is drinking to the point they don't know what they are doing. Keep an open mind, though. Sooner or later truth will be revealed," she proclaimed in her best pulpit voice.

* * *

Sunday morning was sunny but cold. Suzanne
reviewed the sermon which had been snowed out the
week before, and she was ready to speak truth and
invite the congregation to do that also.

All the usual worshipers sat in their places.
Frances, Peter and Julie chose the last pew on the
right near the corner where the storeroom was.
Suzanne no longer thought it strange that people
didn't sit together. The scattered pattern made more
sense now that she knew the seat next to Bertha
wasn't as empty as it looked. Her husband Bob had
always sat there so, of course, no one would take that
seat. It was the same with others. The spirits of the
departed were certainly a reality in that sacred
worship time. *The Communion of Saints, for real.*

The beginning of the service was the same as
always except for the introduction to the Prayer of
Confession. Suzanne foreshadowed her sermon, "If
we say we have no sin, we deceive ourselves, and the
truth is not in us" and went on to talk about the
importance of confession. "One of the signs of evil is
not admitting our sins. If we deny our sins and do not
confess them, they build up. Sins built up can become
a pattern. That pattern is what we call evil."

There was a longer than usual time of silent
confession followed by a short unison prayer.
"Forgive us, God, for times we do wrong and deny
that it is wrong. Forgive us when we fail to tell the
truth."

Suzanne assured them, "We are not stuck.
There is hope, for we have been promised
forgiveness in the name of the Father, Son, and Holy
Spirit. We can begin again at this moment. Amen."

When it was time for the scripture and
sermon, she looked out at the individuals gathered
there and prayed that this was the right thing to do.
Alton sat hunched over, leaning on his cane. She
knew he would be angry with her for bringing this up.

Bertha sat across the aisle from him, eyes closed, face full of peace. She would understand because the focus for this sermon had come out of their conversation about speaking truth to power. Suzanne couldn't predict the others' reactions, but she was glad George wasn't there beside Eva. His face would be red already.

Suzanne repeated that sins if not confessed can become patterns of evil. She quoted scriptures about telling the truth and how we get lazy with the truth. "We need to speak the truth aloud. We need to speak the truth to ourselves. If we lie to ourselves and rationalize what we're doing instead of admitting when we sin, that's when our sins can become habits and patterns. Those patterns of sin become destructive to ourselves and each other and the groups we belong to.

"We need to tell the truth to each other and even take the risk to speak the truth to those in power over us especially when we see those patterns of sin. Our Psalm today talks about telling the glad news of deliverance in the congregation. We here at Harvest look to a time of speaking the glad news of being delivered from what is disrupting our congregation.

"Let's try speaking the truth today." She took a deep breath. "The truth is somebody is hurting the people in this congregation with harassing phone calls and anonymous notes. What else can you say about this that you know is true? I invite you to speak the truth that is in your hearts. Begin with, 'The truth as I see it.'"

Suzanne waited. *If nobody speaks up, what will I say?* Bertha still had her eyes closed. Across the aisle Alton was leaning his forehead on his cane. If he was asleep, she'd never know it. Next to him, Alberta looked down at her hands as though afraid she'd be called on. From the back corner, Frances looked alert and intense, her eyes moving from one person to the other. Peter was writing on a notepad. He didn't look like he was paying attention. Julie looked wide-eyed and a little scared. *I should have prepared them for this.*

Minnie stood up. She turned and faced the congregation. "The truuuth is." She paused to adjust her red beret.

"The truth as I see it," Suzanne prompted.

"The truth, as I see it, is someone is causing grief to people who sure don't need any more grief." She sat down, one hand on her hat.

From the piano bench Tess whispered loud enough for everyone to hear, "I can't take much more of this."

Two sisters were sitting off to one side whispering to each other. They came out from Salina about once a month. Suzanne could tell the older one was getting ready to speak when she sat up straight, set her mouth hard and looked up. She said, "The truth is it's hard to get up in the morning and do a day's work when a body can't get no sleep at night for the phone ringing." Suzanne started to add "as I see it" but decided it was probably a lost cause. *Better to get some responses than to insist on the wording.*

The other sister chimed in, "It's bound to be affecting people's health."

Eva agreed. "The truth is, feeling so angry as some do could cause a stroke."

Alton wasn't asleep on his cane. "The truth is it's only gonna make things worse talking about it," he said without looking up.

Peter stood up. Everyone turned to look at him. Suzanne cringed. His hair was nearly to his shoulders now, but at least it covered the earring in his left ear. He was looking at the picture of Jesus and the lambs. "The truth is I like it here. I like this church."

This couldn't be the same boy who had been fighting with his sister over a pencil just an hour ago.

Does he think I'm saying this isn't a good place? She never expected Peter to speak up, but she hadn't expected so much response from the members either. She paused to see if anyone else looked ready to speak before she summarized.

"We should be careful not to call anyone evil," Alberta said.

"The truth as I see it is," Suzanne tried again.

"It's gotta stop or we're gonna lose our church," Mack said. He was sitting in the back pew on the left, looking up at the ceiling. It was unusual to hear him speak for himself; he usually followed whatever Alton said.

There was a long silence. Suzanne was forming her next words when Bertha spoke up, "The truth, as I see it, is we just want the phone calls and notes to stop. They're all hurtful; but if they'll quit, we won't need to know who's doing this. The truth is we know it's someone we love. I could forgive and go on if they would just stop." Several murmured assent to this.

Minnie spoke from her seat, "We'll always wonder who it is and maybe we can't stop looking around thinking it's one or the other. But I could forgive and go on if we knew who it was and who it wasn't. Pastor, what do you think the truth is?"

Oops, Suzanne thought; *I should have prepared for this.* She started talking before she knew what she was going to say. "You've spoken the truth as you see it. It isn't the same for all of us. But we're trying to speak the truth with each other because we are one with each other as the scriptures teach us. And what hurts one person hurts all of us. And what hurts the congregation as a whole affects each of us. I hadn't thought what else I might say, but then I didn't give you much time to think about it, did I?" There were a couple of smiles. Everyone was looking at her; even Alton had turned his head up, chin on hands. "The truth is," she started. "The truth, as I see it, is that you are the church in this time and place. You worship God together, you take care of each other, and you provide a place where anyone is welcome to come worship with you. And you reach out beyond yourselves to neighbors and people you don't even know, like to help dig wells in the Africa Water Project.

"I'm thinking out loud as I talk," she said. "The truth as I see it." She paused. "The truth I see about the phone calls and notes is that these things are destructive to the goodness of this congregation. They are destructive to individuals, their faith, maybe even their health. The truth, in my mind, is that it's of great importance that this destructiveness stops. Like I said in the sermon, I've been thinking about what I learned from Hans Kung's book <u>The Church</u>. If the Kingdom of God runs through the heart of each of us worshiping here together, then it makes a difference to God's Kingdom when we make choices for what is good or constructive and against what is destructive or evil.

"Anyone else have a truth to speak?" she asked. All eyes were downcast or staring at The Good Shepherd.

She closed with a short prayer. "God of all grace and glory, we lay before you the truth as we see it; and we pledge to seek the truth and speak it to each other. Give us guidance and wisdom, we pray, as we move forward in love. We pray for the one who is disturbing the peace. Help us give that person extra love this day, even as you have loved us. We pray in Jesus' name. Amen."

After the obligatory weather and health conversations in front of the church, Suzanne finally pulled away in the car letting out a long breath, releasing the tension, exhausted yet exhilarated at the same time. However, on the ride home when she least expected it, all the tension came back and her high hopes were dashed.

CHAPTER 37

Reviews

"I wouldn't have gone if I'd known what you were going to do," Peter said. Nobody else said anything for a long time.

Suzanne collected herself and responded as she had been taught. "Tell me more."

"You made the church sound like it was an evil place. It's just like the Salem witch trials we've been reading about at school."

Julie spoke up timidly, "I don't think so."

"What do you know about it, shrimp?"

"It sounds like you feel very angry," Suzanne tried again.

"Don't use that psychology crap on me!"

Suzanne was embarrassed and angry. Her heart started pounding and her breaths came short and shallow. She had expected some feedback about the morning but not this, at least not from her family. Even Alton had shaken her hand at the door, and didn't appear upset, but she would find out at the elders' monthly meeting Wednesday. If he was angry enough, he might even call the Presbytery office and make trouble for her since she hadn't consulted the elders. *But even if they are in charge of the church, nobody is supposed to tell me what to preach. Oh, God, I hope I didn't make things worse.*

Frances was much kinder, but she didn't give Suzanne a hundred per cent approval. "I felt like I was looking in on a family argument. I shouldn't have been there," she said.

Suzanne was quick to respond. "I'm sorry. Were you uncomfortable too, Julie?"

She shrugged. "A little."

"Well," Suzanne said taking a deep breath. "Ya'll tell me more. Tell me the truth."

"First of all," Frances said, "I've learned, the hard way, that when you speak truth to power, you will get a backlash."

"Ahhh," Suzanne sighed. "Of course."

"You need to be prepared for that. Not just aware, but I mean really prepared, with prayer and scripture and maybe even fasting, though that's really taking it seriously." She laughed. "But really, some spiritual practices can bring you closer to God, putting your actions in perspective. I think. . . ." She paused. "I think being prepared like that has helped me at rough times feel less fear and less personal threat. There's something else having to do with motive. Let me think a moment. . . . I guess my purpose becomes clearer and my motives become purer.

"Now," she went on, "from what you said, I don't think anyone will question your motives. There was no self interest evident, and I haven't picked up any in talking with you beyond wanting to succeed. But even that didn't seem very much involved in this. You certainly weren't playing it safe.

"I was shocked that they spoke up so easily in the middle of worship," she said; "but maybe since they are such a small group—. Still, I've never been in a church where people spoke in the worship service if they weren't leading."

"Yeah, you're so high church," Suzanne teased.

"Well, maybe. I've certainly never been in such a small church before. But, of course, more important is what they said. And I was really impressed with what Bertha's comment, 'if the person stops, we'll forgive and go on.' Do you think that could happen?"

"I don't know," Suzanne said. "They are so interwoven and know each other so very well they've probably had to do a lot of forgiving over the years. Either that or they harbor feelings they don't let show. That may be a necessity living as they do so closely with people they've known forever."

"They have to have ways of coping which I can't imagine," Frances said. "Are you sure the person making phone calls was in that room this morning?"

"It has to be one of them or someone they tell about everything that's going on."

"Nobody looked guilty," Frances said. "I was watching, but it didn't seem right for me to be spying on them in the middle of worship."

"Oh," Suzanne said. "Were you able to worship?"

"Well, yes," she said, "and I heard you emphasize that we were there to worship. Telling the truth in the congregation is certainly scriptural, but I was distracted."

"That's not good," Suzanne agreed. "I can see it was awkward for you."

When they pulled into the garage, Peter opened the door and disappeared to the inside before she turned off the ignition.

Suzanne started a fire as Frances continued her thoughts. "It wasn't your fault. I knew what you were going to do. I wonder why I feel this way. I'm sure my anxiety contributed to my discomfort. I was anxious for you and wanted it to go well. But sitting there, I felt real uncomfortable.

"It felt peculiar in other ways, too, other than people speaking up. Many things were missing which I've always associated with worship, particularly the kind of music I'm used to. It left me feeling raw. There was nothing to soothe the roughness of humans together in front of God."

* * *

Suzanne changed into jeans and a sweatshirt then went to look for Peter. She wouldn't stand for him speaking to her that way. Her stomach hurt.

As she started down the stairs, Julie and Peter were running up. "Hey, Mom, we have an idea," Julie said.

"Do you think the church would let us sing on Sundays?" Peter asked.

Suzanne grabbed the handrail and sat down on the stair. "Sing?"

"Yeah, we could work out a duet and . . . would they?" Julie asked.

"They'd love it," Suzanne said. She was breathless. "It's a great idea."

The heart to heart talk would wait. She sat on the stairs resting her head against a spindle.

CHAPTER 38

What Next?

*S*uzanne rushed to the hospital Monday morning. George had suffered what Eva called "a heart flare up." She left Frances alone at the kitchen table with a legal pad in front of her, waiting for phone conversations with her counselor and District Superintendent.

She rode the elevator to the third floor and took deep breaths trying to calm her mind. *Even though George wasn't in church Sunday, he probably knew, along with everybody in the county, that we talked about the phone caller. If he got more calls as a result, this could be my fault.*

It was anybody's guess what will happen next. *If the phone calls became even more insistent, I'll be in what the kids call, "deep doo doo."*

Eva and George didn't mention Sunday. *Of course, even though I can't think of anything else, they have their minds on more important matters.* After a prayer together, George lay snoring in his hospital bed while Eva and Suzanne sat by the window and discussed his condition in whispers.

"He'll be all right," Eva said. As always she gave the impression of great efficiency and got right to the important facts. "He had some arrhythmia but it's stopped and his heart's beating normal-like. They gave him medication, said that's all they'll do except for watching him overnight." Eva finished her report on George's condition and glanced at the book she had in her hand, <u>Iacocca: An Autobiography</u>. That look was a sure sign that she didn't need Suzanne to stay.

* * *

At the church, Suzanne opened the padlock and walked up the wooden stairs to the sanctuary. Her heart raced. In dim light, the pews sat stiffly, the pulpit and communion table were bare, the metal folding chairs in the choir waited, and the picture of Jesus and the lambs looked out on it all from the front wall. In her office, everything was as she had left it.

She turned on the space heater and hoped she'd be spared any phone calls. The task for the day was to decide how to approach the next Sunday. The people might expect a report on whether there was any harassment after they spoke the truth aloud. Maybe they had further thoughts. Or she could give them a chance to say how the week had gone. If talking about it had caused any harm, she needed to know. She could never be absolutely certain what the results of any sermon would be.

When she first started preaching, Suzanne was anxious about every word she said for fear someone would hear wrongly what she meant to say. But there were many times when that happened no matter how careful she was. Once a woman shook her hand at the door and gushed, "I agree completely, Pastor. We should keep that kind of people out of the church."

Shocked, she blurted out, "Oh, no," but the woman moved on, again misunderstanding her.

She recalled expressing her fears to an older pastor. He reminded her that Jesus had the same problem. "Remember how he kept talking about people needing ears to hear?" Then he told her a story about a renowned theologian visiting a village in South America. "The local pastor there interpreted a scripture the opposite of what scholars had all agreed was the meaning, and one of those traveling with the distinguished man asked why he hadn't corrected the pastor. The theologian said, 'The Holy Spirit covers many a well-intentioned word spoken in love to the faithful. Did you not see the white dove flying above our heads?'" Ever since then Suzanne had prayed fervently before every sermon that the dove would show up.

The little office heated up quickly. She turned the thermostat down and looked at her doodles. They were all jagged lines.

When she had her heart-to-heart with Peter about the way he lashed out at her, he mumbled an apology. "I'm just afraid people will start a witch hunt looking for who's evil. I really like that church," he said. "They're not bad people. And I'm not a bad person just because I have a tattoo."

"Peter, I know that. I'll never stop loving you, long hair, tattoo, and all. And I won't stop loving them. I hope they didn't think I was saying that I thought they were bad. And we sure don't want a witch hunt. I'll think about that and watch for their reactions."

She had missed talking with him in depth like that. They had always been close, but they hadn't had a good conversation for some time. He wanted to talk to his dad about everything that came up.

Of course he does. Bell never has disciplined the children. Peter's hair was too long, but Bell wouldn't insist he get it cut. His jeans were ragged at the knee and she said he couldn't wear them. Bell told him to wait and put them on when he got home from school. And the ear ring—well, it was done and so far she hadn't mentioned it to Peter, justifying herself by thinking that what he wanted was a reaction. Nevertheless, she was watching him like a hawk. She worried about him all the time.

She had tried talking to Bell again. "What if this leads to him cutting like that girl in Garry's church?"

"Suzanne, that's totally different. This is self-expression. That's—well, I don't know what that is."

"Right, and we don't know what leads to that kind of behavior. I think Peter's still angry about the move. Bell, listen to me. Your parishioners are going to start talking about this. You'll lose their confidence in you as a role model when their children use your children as an excuse to do these things themselves."

He waved his hand as he turned his back and left the room. "I'm not going to play that game."

She had no control over anything in her life.

* * *

The office cooled off. Her legs felt jumpy. She needed to do something. She wondered if anybody else thought she was instigating a witch hunt. Julie had only said that she didn't hear it that way. Frances was not as concerned about that as she was embarrassed for the people to have dirty laundry aired in public.

Suzanne called Bertha to get her response. Even though someone could listen in, she was willing to take that chance. It might even prove useful for communicating through the grapevine.

"Pastor," Bertha said when Suzanne shared her concern, "I thought it went really well. We've never spoken that way with each other, all of us together saying what is true. I felt a great relief just having the words said out loud."

"Oh, good." Suzanne let out a sigh. "I'm preparing next week's sermon and trying to figure out what people heard and what their responses were so I know where to go from here."

"Well, I can't say what others thought, nobody's talked to me about it," Bertha said, "but now that I think on it, I suppose, like you said, someone could start looking for an evil person. Yes, I think that could happen. Could you tell us more about how to recognize evil? And I guess we need to know what to do once we see it for what it is."

Suzanne closed her eyes thinking about the phone conversation and swung this way and that in her swivel chair, passing one leg then the other in front of the space heater. She knew it was a shock to hear the word "evil" used in a concrete way about current happenings. She remembered when in a continuing education seminar the presenter had described the characteristics of evil and how important it was for us to see it in ourselves and stop shying away from calling it by name. The surprise was that she hadn't realized that "evil" as a present reality had been kicked to the sidelines in mainline churches. That had probably happened in response to the image of a red man with a spiked tail and pitchfork who was used to scare little children into doing right. She had always thought that if the focus stayed on love and justice, less power would be given to what was destructive. But that seminar opened her eyes to the need to name evil and stand up to it. The cautions were helpful too: don't get mesmerized by evil, don't fight evil with evil. *Don't start witch hunts,* she mentally added, trying to remember if that had been mentioned.

It had, of course, been risky to open up the subject, as had been pointed out to her by those she loved. It was true, the minute anyone started pointing the finger at evil, a whole firestorm erupted, either backlash from the evil itself or a witch hunt for someone to blame. It was a dilemma. Certainly in the church they needed to talk about evil, but she hoped she hadn't opened Pandora's Box. This would be good to discuss with the clergy. Until she could do that, she was on her own. She felt the familiar panic that came when she had to stretch into areas she felt little competence to speak about.

It would certainly be easier to ignore what was going on and stick to telling the stories of the Bible without applying them. I don't know why I do this to myself. She had thought she was on solid ground in the last sermon, but now she was being pushed into clarifying in practical terms a subject which was full of land mines. *Surely I can find a way to describe the characteristics of evil again with different illustrations and then look at ways to respond.*

She reviewed her file notes from the seminar and found several scriptures which illustrate different ways to deal with evil. Herod killed all the children younger than two years of age, trying to do away with the child the wise men said was born King of the Jews. In response Joseph and Mary avoided this evil by escaping to Egypt with their baby Jesus. Avoidance. Yes, sometimes that was the best choice. Deal with evil by avoiding it.

What else? Jesus in the wilderness tempted to use his power in wrong ways. He made good choices. Good choices.

Jesus in the Garden of Gethsemane. They came to arrest him and Peter pulled out a sword. But Jesus told him that those who live by the sword would die by the sword. Elsewhere he had said to love your enemies and do good to those who hurt you. Resist evil by an act of love, never by warfare. Sounds like nonviolent resistance. That would need to be presented in a clear and direct way without getting distracted by current political debates. A response of love.

Jesus on the cross. That was the ultimate way to address evil. A loving sacrifice.

This was getting deep and complex. She would have to distill it into concepts and words which would communicate to them. It was too much for one sermon.

She could start with the Salem Witch Trials to caution against a witch hunt. It would be necessary to tell the whole story. She knew not to assume they had what she thought of as common knowledge.

She had learned that most of the people in Harvest were old enough not to have a background in psychology, not even knowing what a Freudian slip was when she had used that phrase. And television was a fairly new phenomenon for them.. Only in the past few years had television signals reached them. So she had learned not to use examples and illustrations from television shows or psychology.

She went on dreaming and planning. The office grew warm. The heater shut off. She leaned back in her chair and propped her feet up on a drawer of the desk. The silence was full. She let her mind float.

She grew cold and reached over to turn the thermostat on the heater. It wouldn't budge. She used both hands to force it to move. Nothing. Jesus walked in the door holding a newborn lamb, its eyes still closed. He touched the heater and it began warming. He laid his hand on Suzanne's head in a blessing. She felt a profound peace which lasted even when he left the room.

"Pastor?"

She awoke with a start, nearly turning the chair over. Grady and Lassie stood in the doorway. "Sorry to disturb you," he said. "I came to see if everything was all right. The power's out."

"Oh, yes," she said, startled out of the peaceful scene. Lassie put his head on her knee and looked at her with intelligent, friendly eyes. Suzanne communed with him in pats and murmurs.

"Thanks, I'd better finish up at home," she said. "How are things at your house?"

"We're fine, and I checked on Bertha and Minnie. They've got enough wood cut. Everybody out here has a fireplace. The wind blowing like it does we have lines down all the time so we have to stay prepared."

"Okay, well, I'll be getting on then. Thanks for checking on me." She started gathering her notes. Grady turned to leave and Lassie followed. He glanced at his painting of The Shepherd.

"Grady, I can't tell you how much that painting comforts me."

He went on as though he hadn't heard her.

CHAPTER 39

Who Could It Be?

*W*hen Suzanne got home, Frances was packing. "Chet called. He wants me to come home and work things out. He said that . . . that . . . girl listened to him and seemed to understand how he was being pulled apart." She was trying to fold a sweatshirt but gave up and stuffed it in her duffle bag. "He said they never . . . ."

Suzanne was puzzled. "Oh, you mean . . . ?"

"Sex," Frances said. "He said . . . but I don't know if I believe that. He can't go more than three days without."

"Three days!" It just popped out. Frances looked up at her questioningly but neither one said more. As well as they knew each other, they had never talked about their sex lives. Suzanne wondered what was normal.

Frances talked frantically as she packed. "The D.S. is going to try to move us to separate churches, solo pastorates, so we can support each other without those inevitable congregational dynamics driving a wedge between us."

Frances was obviously excited to go home. "Bell said he'd take me if you can't. We need to leave right away to make the flight."

* * *

Suzanne concentrated on driving through the light rain while Frances talked. "He's going to meet me at the airport. I don't know what I'll say. Maybe I'll just fall into his arms in tears. No, no, I don't want to do that. Maybe I'll be cool and distant. Hmmm, I don't think I can pull that off."

Her excited chatter wound down, and she was quiet. Suzanne let the silence hold. The energy in the car was tamped down by the rhythm of the windshield wipers and the monotonous stretches of fields speeding past them.

After a while Frances said, "Well, we haven't solved The Mystery of Harvest, Kansas, yet. Do you have a feeling about who's behind all the trouble?"

"No," Suzanne said, "my strongest intuition says there's nobody that hateful; yet my logic says it has to be one of them."

"Is there anyone you haven't gotten to know yet? Maybe it's someone very quiet who feels left out."

"That would make sense. Someone might resent those who are active and target them. I keep thinking there has to be that kind of motive, and then I get stumped. Nobody is left out that I can see. I've made a significant contact with each person and still have no clue. Of course, you never really know what's going on in a person's head.

"Whoever wrote those notes has to be there most of the time for worship and for activities in order to know what's going on. I assume it's a woman, but it could be a man who has disguised his voice."

"How many people come to everything?" Frances asked.

"There are sixteen who are there for most every worship service and activity, and I took off the list anyone who wasn't at the Chicken Noodle Supper and anyone who wasn't in church the Sunday Peter wore jeans. I took out those who received notes. That's Alton and Alberta, Minnie, Eva and George, Tess and Grady. Then I took off everyone who got phone calls when I was with them. That's Bertha, Eva and George. After that, I was left with no one on the list except Mack, but he was targeted in the notes.

"There's so much I don't know about them. I'm becoming aware of the long history they have. Something from way back could have led to this moment. Alton told me that there are people who still won't speak to him because he was on the school board when they voted to consolidate. That was a long time ago. All the kids from Harvest and Gypsum and other small towns around here go to a new school called Southeast of Saline. When they lost their local school, I guess they saw it as the end of Harvest.

"The older generation remembers when all the little towns were rivals in sports, and now their children are in the same school. It is hard for some of them to accept it. There could be some grudge like that behind this. Still, as far as I can see, nothing makes sense. It's not just one person who's being targeted, it's the whole church."

Frances checked her face in the passenger mirror. "I've been thinking that your assumptions could be flawed. For instance, someone could have sent themselves a note along with sending one to other people or said something about themselves in the notes. And about those phone calls—there could be a malfunction in the system which makes the phones ring like they do. It also could be more than one person making calls."

Suzanne laughed. "Well, now that you mention it, all that is possible. If so, it's no wonder they haven't been able to figure it out."

"Now you're thinking," Frances said hooting with laughter, "and you're back to it being about almost anyone instead of no one."

"You're a lot of help."

They were quiet for a while. The rain picked up and the wheels made a steady swish on the wet highway. Then Frances said, "One thing we know for sure. It's not a person they would expect to do this kind of thing. If it were simple to figure out, they would have done that a long time ago."

"Yes," Suzanne said tapping the steering wheel, "they used to think it was a woman named Melba so they hadn't been looking around at each other until recently—at least concerning the phone calls. But she died and the calls continued. She was too feeble to be doing it anyway, and there was no way she could cause the trouble inside the church building. "

"Try looking at it differently," Frances suggested. "Instead of thinking why it couldn't be each one of them, tell me some reason why it could be a person nobody would expect—like Bertha. Make something up. Imagine a reason."

"That's hard," Suzanne said. "I know it's not her. But let's see. She is the least likely person so she'd be overlooked by everyone."

"Good, now give her a reason."

"It would have to be a split personality. And her kind side wouldn't know the other side was acting out."

"Okay, that's good," Frances said. "Pick another person."

"Mack. Let's say he's taking money, and trying to throw attention elsewhere, though I can't imagine how that could be true."

"That's okay," Frances said. "This will open your mind. Next."

"Minnie. She's overmedicated and doesn't know what she's doing.

"Eva. She's covering for George.

"George. He's angry, retaliating against someone.

"Grady. Passive anger, grief.

"Tess. She's had so much abuse, she's trying to get back at someone.

"Junior. I don't know. I know so little about him. And I've tried.

"Alberta. She's the boss, likes to tell people how to do things right. And I think she would cover for Alton.

"Alton. He's been most against trying to figure out what's going on. He could be covering for Alberta or himself. He did say people resented them having the biggest farm around.

I can see this is opening my mind up, but it's also going to make me more suspicious of everyone," Suzanne said.

"Maybe someone wants the church to close,. Who would benefit from that?" Frances asked.

"I don't know of anyone."

They had to leave it at that. Traffic picked up. They went through the toll booth and neared the airport. "Frances, thanks for thinking about my church. We haven't talked about your situation nearly as much as I thought we would."

"You gave me every opportunity. It was just right, as I knew it would be. It's a blessing to have good friends who understand that you need distraction, comfort, and space to think. Thank you, thank you. Tell the kids goodbye for me."

Suzanne hugged her goodbye. "I'll pray for your peace and Chet's. I hope you'll find your way clear." She brushed away a tear.

CHAPTER 40

Elders' Meeting

The elders met for their monthly meeting on Wednesday night at Mack's; and at his request, Suzanne arrived early. All along the road emerald green fields stood proudly. Some of those fields had weeds sticking up here and there, but not Mack's. His had no breaks in the flat surface. She imagined lying down on top, tiny green fingers holding her up.

She had been in Mack's barn but never his home. Shortly after Bell and the children had been to his farm to ride the tractor, Suzanne met the animals Julie had been so excited about.

Mack called each one of them by name and talked baby talk to them. "Here, Sookie, hey, Poochy, we got company," he had called to a large sow and an aging goat. "Some was Mama's pets," he had told her, tenderly picking up a piglet. "These're their offspring. Kinda keeps Mama alive for me.

"She and Dad passed on a few years back," he told her on that first visit. "When I was just a kid, they bought this land and moved here from Lindsborg so she could have animals and Dad could grow wheat. Junior's parents bought part of it later on. He farms over yonder." He pointed south to a row of scrub trees. "We help each other out since we don't have no relations here no more. People call us 'outliers.' Most people out here are related to each other somewheres back. Not that they've treated me bad. The neighbors and church people have sure been good to me."

He told her in great detail about his broken ankle and how people did his chores and brought him meals for weeks until he could get around and do for himself. "Best food I'd had since Mama died. I ain't much of a cook."

Suzanne felt affection for this roughhewn man. She would never have guessed from his unpolished ways, the way he cleaned his fingernails with a pocket knife and yawned openly throughout the church service, that he had such a warm and tender heart.

There is no way Mack could be responsible for the trouble but then I've said that about each one of those dear people. Nevertheless, it is one of them, and I'll be sad to find out who.

Now as she faced the house, dirty white with one shutter askew and a sheet of plastic taped over the front window, she realized what a contrast it was to the freshly painted white barn. It was clear where his priorities lay. Next to the barn, covered by a doorless lean-to shed, his shiny, green tractor glowed proudly.

Mack stepped out of the back door to greet her, wiping his hands on a gray dish towel. Those stained hands of his always looked as though he had been digging in the ground or working on machinery. His John Deere cap, ragged around the brim, sat firmly in place as it always did except in church. Tonight he wore his usual overalls with a white tee shirt underneath. Both were creased, no doubt new and just removed from their packaging.

She followed him through the kitchen door which slammed behind her. The aroma of old bacon grease reminded her of her grandmother's farmhouse.

In the dining room five chairs were pulled up to the mahogany table and Mack was in the process of moving stacks of magazines, newspapers and mail from the table to the floor under the window.

He pulled his treasurer's ledger from the roll top desk next to the stacks. She remembered this red and gray book. He had brought it to church to show her how he kept track of the church's income and expenses. His neatly penciled entries were beautiful in their simplicity and precision.

No doubt someone had told him about the notes. She braced herself for his defense, but it quickly became clear that he didn't have that on his mind. She was sitting down and placing her glass on a piece of notebook paper when he began, "Pastor, I asked you to come early to tell you it's not Grady been causing the mischief."

Mack sat down at the table and went on, "I thought I ought to tell you, in case you found out, that Grady was in the church lots of times at night. He's a walker, walks all over the county, any kind of weather. And sometimes I seen him at the church real late when I come home from Salina the back way. A few times I stopped when I saw a light on in the church. It was the spot light over the big picture. I looked in and seen him sitting up there on one of them chairs looking at Jesus. He'd just be staring at it. For a while, if I saw a light on, I'd stop and check on him to be sure he was all right. I kindly worried that—well, that he couldn't take it any more." Mack stumbled over his words. "Th – then I decided that he wasn't gonna hurt himself or nothing and I stopped looking in. I think sitting in the church at night with his picture helps him get through so I didn't worry about him no more, just let him be. He'd probably never do anything, you know, foolish. Ever since I knowed him he's been a real religious person, though he don't talk about it much."

Suzanne tried to piece together what Mack was saying. "So Grady's the one who's been in the church at night? Do you think he might have been the one who wadded up the communion cloth?"

"No," Mack said softly as he pushed himself up to go let the others in the kitchen door. "He couldn't never do that, and he ain't the one been sending notes neither."

Mack began before Suzanne could call the meeting to order. "We gotta put a stop to this meanness. If we don't, we're gonna end up without a church."

Alton was quick to counter his anxiety. "Now Mack, don't nobody worry about you being treasurer. This is just some mischief-making, don't take it personal like. Did you hear about the treasurer over in Smolan? Told his church he had to quit. Been doing it for years and nobody could figure out why he would stop now. They worried he was sick or something. Finally, he got tired of their questions and told them, 'I can't keep making up the shortfall.'" Alton laughed, wheezing and coughing. "He thought the treasurer had to pay the bills when there weren't enough money in the plate."

Eva and Junior laughed politely. Even Mack smiled. *They've heard this before*, Suzanne thought.

After opening the meeting with prayer, Suzanne asked Alton to read the minutes of the previous meeting. He did and proudly showed them the record book all up to date.

At Mack's request, she reviewed with them the contents of the notes received and asked for discussion. "Don't even think about stopping those children," Eva said. "And wearing jeans is just fine."

"And we don't pay any attention to that there about you, Mack" Alton said. "The part about Tess neither."

"Isn't there some way to stop this?" Junior asked.

Eva answered, "We need to do something about all this aggravation, but I've reached the end of my rope trying to think how."

Suzanne asked for any ideas and waited for someone to mention her sermon. She was still wondering if it had caused more trouble or had any positive effect.

"We tried tapping the phone long time ago," Alton said. "Could try it again."

"I'm not sure what good that would do what with our party lines," Eva said. "We'd get down to six like before and still not be sure. And anyway, who's to say that the very call we tap is a mischief one. It could be legitimate." "We could keep track of who's not around when we get the calls," Mack said.

Eva was quick to respond, "We try to do that, but it don't get us nowhere. It used to point to one person. We all thought we knew who it was but didn't want to hurt her feelings. Now she's gone and the calls don't come when any of us are together."

"Have there been any calls or notes since we talked openly in church Sunday?" Suzanne asked.

"No, but that's not gonna stop them," Alton said. He didn't add that it would make them worse, but Suzanne suspected he was thinking that.

"From what you're saying, it sounds like the phone calls are more bothersome than the notes or somebody fooling around inside the church," Suzanne said. All nodded so she went on, "A pastor friend of mine recommended I talk to a man he knows at the phone company. He says the man can be trusted to keep this confidential. What do you think about my consulting him? Maybe there's something wrong in the lines that would cause the phone to ring like it does. I could ask him if that's possible and also see if he has any advice."

They agreed with this plan of action and Suzanne assured them she would not set up a phone tap unless they all agreed to do it.

Alton surprised her by disagreeing. "You know, Alberta says this has caused too much grief especially for Grady and Tess so I'd say go ahead and follow through on whatever they tell you. No need to come back to us as far as I'm concerned. I guess we got to do something now that everybody's talking about it."

CHAPTER 41

The Phone Company

Suzanne sat across a mahogany table from Robert Sullivan. His office at the phone company was spacious and furnished with antiques. A handsome navy suit hung perfectly on his long, lean frame; and his soft white hair begged to be touched. The white was obviously premature for his age but it gave him an aura of competence. At first she prepared herself to be dealt with quickly and efficiently; but as she told him about their phone problems, his warm gray eyes showed undivided attention. With a little encouragement she told him how the persistent ringing of phones was driving her parishioners crazy, and their attempts to get it to stop weren't working.

Mr. Sullivan tried to be helpful. "There's no way a malfunction could cause the phones to ring like that. In a few years we'll have a way to call back on a hang up and find out who placed the call, but for now all we can do is put a tap on the line. That would at least narrow down to those sharing the party line. The first step is to file a complaint with the police department or sheriff. You have to agree to prosecute when the person abusing the phone system is found. We can't do anything without that formal complaint."

"This is a small and close-knit community," she explained. "Everybody's related to everybody, and I am hesitant to do anything which will set off a chain reaction of destruction. If we end up pointing a finger at someone without being absolutely sure, that's what will happen."

"I understand. Tell the sheriff that. See if he'll work with you."

* * *

Sheriff Weller sat with his feet up on a corner of his desk and chewed on a toothpick, moving it in time to the music on the radio. "Hear that train a comin." He cut to the bottom line very quickly. "Either you want to do this or you don't. Why don't you sign all the papers, think about it and call me when you're ready to proceed. If you decide not to pursue it, I'll tear them up. You know, if a tap goes to a party line, it'll only narrow the field to all those on that line so from that alone, prosecution would be highly unlikely."

Thinking quickly and relieved that prosecution would be virtually impossible; she went ahead, signed the papers and told him to proceed.

"I am concerned that investigating one person could have unfortunate repercussions in that close community."

"I understand. Got just the deputy for that," he said. "Renfro knows the people out there."

Then she worried about it the rest of the day. Prosecution wasn't at all what the church would want. She was sure of that. She talked it over with Bell. "What I want is to find out who it is so I can work with the person; maybe we could go forward in a constructive way. After all reconciliation is what we're all about."

Bell listened to her concerns, but his advice was noncommittal. "Sweetheart, you know best on this. I don't have a clue."

She wrote in her book that night before going to sleep:

> Best possible scenario:
> Find out who is harassing.
>
> Manage the healing process for the congregation. Tell them it's over, the person is getting help, no name to be given unless the person wants to ask forgiveness.
>
> Encourage the congregation to give that forgiveness even if they don't know who it is.
>
> If the person is prosecuted, get the Presbytery Executive and the Presbytery's lawyer involved.
>
> I stay in the pastoring role.
>
> Stay close to each person including the guilty one. Offer care and support.

It could happen that way, she thought. *It's a long shot, but it could happen.*

CHAPTER 42

Accusations

*O*n Friday Suzanne finally had time to look at the sermon notes she'd made on Monday. Now they fell into a neat outline.

WEEK 1
I. Repeat definition and characteristics of sin and evil
    A. Turning from God, using people as things
    B. Destructiveness
    C. Confusion, lies, lack of repentance and confession
    D. Continuing in the pattern
       WEEK 2
II. Cautions about naming sin and evil
    A. Salem Witch Trial account
    B. The eighth deadly sin, seeing sin where there is none
    C. Backlash possibilities, preparation
III. Ways of Responding
    A. Turn a blind eye. "Evil will prevail when good people do nothing."
       WEEK 3
    B. Avoid. Escape to Egypt with baby Jesus
    C. Make good choices, resist evil. Jesus' temptations

WEEK 4

D. Return good for evil. Turn the other
cheek

WEEK 5

E. Make a sacrifice of love to God in the face
of evil.

GOOD FRIDAY. The cross.

IV. God redeems evil. Look for the resulting good.

EASTER. Resurrection

She studied the scriptures more thoroughly
and made some notes, but Sunday's sermon was far
from written. She hoped to finish it and have
Saturday free, but there were too many interruptions.

First Danny Canny stopped by the church.
She heard his precisely measured footsteps and the
swing of the sanctuary doors. "Pastor?" he called in
an artificially deep voice.

She welcomed him into her office thinking
again that they should figure a way to lock the front
doors when she was there alone. Right now the
padlock was on the outside so it was a fire hazard to
lock it if anyone was in the building.

Suzanne gritted her teeth. He pulled his left
pant leg up from the knee as he sat down affecting a
mannerism no doubt seen in a movie. It lost its effect
since his old black suit was limp, no crisp pleat there.
Without any pleasantries, he opened a thick photo
album on her desk covering up her notes. "I want to
show you something."

On the first page was his grandmother's
picture and across from it her obituary. Next was his
grandfather. Then their siblings were similarly laid
out, picture and obituary, picture and obituary. He
simply identified each one until he came to his
parents and their siblings. He began to tell her facts
turning each page without emotion. "This is my Aunt
Belle, Mother's sister. She took her own life. Here is

my cousin Harry. He died of a heart attack at age 34."
Then it got really bizarre. "My uncle Byron, Dad's
brother killed his wife and then himself." They had
posed on a happier day in wedding clothes and
surrounded by flowers. He went on, now describing
his father's step sister who killed her two children.
Little faces beamed from the page. Next was a picture
of a young boy with a cowlick and big teeth. "My best
friend Tommy, fourth grade, he was killed by a train."
On and on it went, a litany of loss until the pages
were empty, waiting. He flipped to the back. The last
one held his own picture. He stared at it. The
heaviness she felt around him now had a name.
Death, death pulls at his feet. No, maybe it's not
death but life that pulls him down, the pain of life.
Grief.

"Oh, Danny," she said. He jumped as though
he had forgotten she was there. It became apparent
he wasn't looking for sympathy when he turned back
to the page showing a short, rotund man, his chest
stuck out in pride, standing beside a sign, "Cosby-
Canny Funeral Parlor."

He pointed to the picture. "My father was a
good man." He paused, a dramatic pause. "Yesterday
my cousin Renfro came to ask me about the trouble
you're having here."

"What—" Suzanne began, but he cut her off.

"Renfro. He's a new deputy, and since he's
from out here, the sheriff assigned him to the case."

"Oh, no," Suzanne said. "He shouldn't go
around talking to people about this. That's not going
to help. Rumors will start and people will be hurt.
The church will be hurt."

"Now, now," he said. "It was just me. He's
my cousin and he knows I'm well-informed about
everything going on. His mother was my Aunt Belle."
He flipped back to her picture. *Suicide,* Suzanne
remembered.

"Anyway, Renfro knows the history out here, and he agreed that I should tell you about George. If there's trouble you can be sure he's behind it. He's the meanest person I ever met and his daddy was meaner than him." Suzanne tried to think which one in the gallery of death was George. Then she realized he was talking about Eva's George.

"When my dad and George's dad were in high school, my dad got a car. George's dad was so jealous, he started bullying my dad. Beat him up pretty bad one time. Later, when they were both married and had children—now, I actually remember this, I was 12 years old—he started rumors, telling people my dad fooled around with corpses. You know, did stuff with them. It was sick. He was evil, just plain evil. I don't know how George's mother stood it. I don't know how Eva stands it now because George is just like his dad, flying into a rage at the least provocation and then . . . then, well, no telling what will happen. I hear tell George's dad killed a man once and somehow got away with it.

"Well, anyway, the people of this town knew my dad. He was the biggest contributor to the Methodist Church, and the pastor was at our table most Sundays for dinner. And everybody knew how mean George's dad was so it didn't ruin us. But, you know, a rumor like that in a small community could wipe out a person's business.

"Now, I'm telling you this and I told Renfro, too. Mark my words. If that church closes, I'll bet you the land will go to George. It started out as part of his family's."

Suzanne broke in, "I've been there when George got calls." .

His eyes bulged, his jaw dropped. He sat there staring.

Suzanne wanted out. He'd come in there accusing one of her members without any proof, keeping a family feud going. She thought about asking him to leave. But she hesitated. He was awkward, probably lonely. This was not the first time she had sat and listened to more than she wanted to hear from someone. She couldn't turn him away. She sensed his despair, caught up in a web of death over several generations. Still, he shouldn't go around accusing someone without proof and calling a person evil without careful consideration of the facts and the repercussions.

"I'll bet you anything it's George causing trouble," Danny said. "There was this woman down in Wichita who was being harassed by nasty notes. They finally found out she was writing the notes herself. George is the one complaining most. He fits the picture." Finally, he closed the album and walked out, like a referee leaving the field after making the call.

Suzanne knew though that George had received phone calls himself. She had been there. She had seen his red face. She had also been irritated at the interruptions.

It was only minutes later she heard labored footsteps on the stairs. "Yoo-hoo."

It was Minnie. She wanted to talk. Bell would say, "The flood gates have opened."

"People tell you things," he had said to her more than once over the years. "How do you get them to do that? People never tell me all that kind of thing about their lives."

"I don't do anything," she told him. "I don't try to get them to tell me their deepest secrets."

Minnie wasn't flouncing today. She was rather subdued. She sat on the folding chair Danny had just left and stared at the floor. "I want to tell you something." Suzanne waited. "It's about George," she whispered. "He's the one making phone calls. I heard Eva in the background one time."

"But, Minnie, I was at his house when he got calls," Suzanne said repeating what she had told Danny and wondering how this could happen that two people would be accusing George on the same afternoon.

"Well," she went on, still looking at the floor, her voice even softer. "Sometimes after I get a lot of them, I give him a dose of his own medicine."

"A dose of his own medicine." George said that. In The Café he said those very words.

"Who else have you called," Suzanne asked evenly.

"Oh, no one." Her head jerked up, and she looked Suzanne in the eyes. "No, I just wanted George to know what it felt like."

"Minnie, I've received calls here, too."

"Must be George," she said.

CHAPTER 43

Lent

*D*uring the six weeks of Lent, Suzanne found it difficult to find time for meditation and self-examination. She did sit in a pew each morning, reading a Psalm and enjoying the silence, but it was difficult to escape her tumbling thoughts and the phone ringing. The more she tried to empty her mind, the more frustrated she got, so she gave up and let her thoughts roam.

Occasionally she fell asleep but didn't chastise herself. More than once she had told a sleepy soul, who apologized for sleeping in church, that sometimes a body needed to fall asleep in God's arms.

Her thoughts often returned to George and Minnie. They might be calling each other, but somebody else was calling, too. *Surely neither of them would call me to "administer a dose of their own medicine" unless they think I'm making prank calls.*

The phone tap was scheduled. It would come during the week before Easter. As far as she could tell the sermon series on evil was going well, and plans for Easter week were coming together.

Julie caught her by surprise one day. "Do you know you're sighing again?" That was a sure sign she needed to relax; but she had trouble concentrating enough to follow relaxation techniques so she kept on putting one foot in front of the other, planning worship services and trying to figure out what was going on around her.

Peter still worried her, but Bell said, "Don't worry about him. His grades are still real good; and, after all, he's going to church every Sunday."

The highlight of every week was Julie and Peter's duet in church. They sang without accompaniment, voices blending beautifully. Usually they didn't plan what they were singing until Saturday night when they'd ask what the sermon topic was. Then they'd look through the hymnal for a song that fit. Each Sunday the congregation members surrounded them after worship asking them to please sing again next week. One Sunday on the way home Peter said, "When we sing, they don't seem so sad."

There were occasional moments like that when she could glimpse the old Peter. However, most often he was sullen, and if he did speak to her it was in one syllable words. He acted like he hated her. It broke her heart.

The phone calls were more frequent during the weeks of Lent, much more numerous at the office and sometimes even disturbing them at home. Tess said she and Grady were even getting calls in the middle of the night. Suzanne wondered if her own family was getting more calls because Peter and Julie were singing on Sunday mornings. Each time the phone rang, Julie would say, "That may be our friend, say a prayer for her."

Suzanne let Dr. Talley know what was going on and was relieved that he didn't press her to do anything differently. "Just keep us informed," he said. There was also a committee of the Presbytery charged with overseeing conflicts in churches so she let them know about the phone tap and what was going on, a little protection for her in case things blew up.

Thinking it all over, once again, she wondered why she had been called by God to Harvest, if indeed it was God's call. *The church will probably close in the next few years. It's most likely that in the end all anyone can do is help them celebrate their church's life over the years and close the doors. Those good folks can then go on to healthier congregations where they can be the church without constant distractions.*

I certainly didn't need four years of college and three of seminary to do this. Why, God, why am I not in a place where I can use all I learned? This feels like exile. Or abandonment. She sighed. All she knew to do was keep on keeping on, one day at a time.

* * *

The clergy group was always interested and supportive. At one meeting Suzanne let off steam. "This is taking us away from what is important. Some days I think it will never end. I get angry with them and then angry with myself for being angry because it's not all of them. It's probably just one or well, maybe two or three. And I keep working it over in my mind," she said, "trying to find a way for us to be healthy together and heal this situation so we can go on being the church. It's sucking all the energy and spirit right out of us. I just want us all to be happy."

Bell chuckled. "Isn't that your birthday wish every time you blow out the candles, that we all be happy?"

She ducked her head. "Well, yes, ever since I was a child. Of course, being happy means something different now. It's more complex, but it's still my wish."

"Suze, the situation at Harvest is difficult," Bell said. "I have no idea how to solve their difficulties; but if anyone can do it, you can. You're really good at everything you do and I don't know anyone better at creative problem solving."

"Thanks, Bell, but I can't find a place to start. I really don't know what I'm doing. It's possible that Alton was right. He's seen so much in that community. Maybe, like he says, it's the kind of thing which needs to be handled by ignoring it. That's the way we've been taught to deal with anonymous notes and letters. Perhaps the principle is the same. I sure don't know how to use conflict management techniques when one party is missing. But I'm discovering that these people handle things in very different ways from the larger churches I've been in."

They reassured her she was doing the best she could and they saw no other way to go; but deep in her heart Alton's warning still rang like an alarm bell, "No good will come of talking about this. You'll stir things up. Just keep quiet about it." And now Deputy Renfro had talked to Danny Canny and who knew how many others.

* * *

That afternoon she called Deputy Renfro. He was cordial and seemed to understand her concerns. "I grew up out there, Pastor; I know what you're talking about. I'll do my best to keep from doing more harm than good as we try to figure out what's going on. Feel free to call me any time day or night if you have trouble." He gave her his home number.

"He sounds very young," she told Bell. "I won't be calling him except as a last resort."

CHAPTER 44

The Phone Tap

*I*t was hard to tell exactly what would generate the phone ringing more on one day than another. It may have been coincidence, but after the sermon about returning good for evil, nonstop calls came into the church office. Suzanne suggested to the congregation that they follow Julie's lead and every time they got a phone call pray for the person on the other end before answering it, no matter who it was. "And if no one is there, whisper a prayer into the phone. It's a way to take back your power and use it for good."

It was actually a relief that the phone caller was active the Monday before Easter because the phone tap was set for the next day. For once, Suzanne hoped the calls would continue. As she was packing up to go home that afternoon a different call came. She let it ring a while and then lifted the handset without saying anything. Then there was someone there, male or female she couldn't tell. The sound was distorted by something, perhaps paper over the mouthpiece.

"Stop it. I don't want your prayers," the voice hissed.

"I will not stop," Suzanne said. She kept her voice calm and sent waves of peace toward the caller.

This was not simply a prank call. Prayer was disturbing her . . . or him and whatever was going on went deeper than a grudge against a few people.

God, protect us all, this disturbed and disturbing person, those who receive the phone calls and the person from the phone company who will figure out who it is tomorrow.

On the way home, she felt sick at her stomach. She recognized it as a sign of fear, but she sent it away. "I will not stop. You will not destroy these good people!" she said out loud.

* * *

The next day, the Tuesday before Easter a man from the phone company went to the concrete block building off the road to Gypsum and waited. Suzanne hoped for his sake that a call came early so he wouldn't have to sit there all day. A few minutes after ten Suzanne's office phone rang, and when she answered, no one was there. She left the phone off the hook and drove down the road to tell the man she had done so. He said it would take a few days for her to get the information.

Then what will we do? she wondered.

CHAPTER 45

Easter

*E*aster morning was warm and idyllic. The sun's rays shone through fluffy clouds lined up in layers. All their bottoms made flat lines across the sky. A few brave daffodils dressed the road to Harvest in yellow.

As they drove to church, Julie and Peter practiced sang, "Every Morning is Easter Morning," and Suzanne thought through her sermon. The theme matched the way she felt, full of hope and possibilities for life.

After the phone tap there were no more calls so Holy Week was peaceful. On Maundy Thursday evening the worship service had claimed the sanctuary as sacred space like nothing else could. They remembered the Last Supper, Jesus' arrest in the Garden of Gethsemane, and the trial and crucifixion. A black cloth was draped over the picture of Jesus, and candles filled the room. After each of Jesus' last words Alberta extinguished a few candles until the only light in the room was one little candle on the communion table. "Even in the darkest night, there is always hope," the people proclaimed.

In those holy moments, in the face of the ultimate sacrifice of love, the little irritations in Harvest faded. Suzanne had left the church that night thinking of the many times in history when people had held on tightly to God and each other when they didn't know what to do to save themselves.

Now she walked into the silence of the church ready for joyful music and the fragrance of Easter lilies. The first thing she saw was the communion table lying on its side. She found the white cloth wadded up and stuffed in among the choir chairs as they had told her happened once before. The lilies were dumped on the floor, water running down under the piano.

Julie discovered the banner was slashed. It was new, a gift from Bertha on the occasion of her granddaughter's baptism scheduled for that morning. On a navy blue background, little round people walked a white road which wandered from bottom to top. Words at the top proclaimed, "I have called you by name."

It was slashed up the middle. A butcher knife lay on the floor. Suzanne retrieved it and put it out of sight in her office. Eva came in and set her face in a stoic mask. She disappeared into the basement and came back with needle and thread. Without a word, she set about stitching it together in a neat seam as Julie held it together for her.

Minnie found the Communion bread in the kitchen garbage and the juice poured out in the sink. She went back home and returned with cookies and prune juice, lending a little levity to the situation.

Suzanne was most upset to see the pulpit Bible had "lies" written on the front in red marker. She clasped it to her then placed it on one of the throne chairs.

Her heart was heavy. Nevertheless, they celebrated Easter Sunday. She looked out at her little flock. Everyone was there for this Holy day. *Which one of you is it?* she wondered. Then she pushed her own anger down and clamped a seal on it, pulling herself together and concentrating on making this a worshipful and joyful day in spite of the anger in the room.

They did worship. They baptized Mary who with her mother answered the questions about what they believed. One of the first questions took on a real and present meaning to all in the room.

"Trusting in the gracious mercy of God, do you turn from the ways of sin and renounce evil and its power in the world?"

After church the elders gathered at the pulpit and agreed that they had to do whatever it took to stop this. Suzanne called Deputy Renfro and waited for him. Bertha offered to drop Julie and Peter off at home when she went into Salina for Easter dinner with her daughter and granddaughter.

Suzanne sat on the front steps of the church in the sunshine waiting for Renfro and wondering what this would lead to and how she should proceed.

Renfro brought a crew to dust for fingerprints. "You're sure nobody but you touched the Bible and the knife?"

"Yes, but what will you do if you get good fingerprints?" Suzanne asked. "How would you—?"

"We'll have to get all your members fingerprinted and then isolate your prints from any others on the knife and the Bible?"

"Oh, no—" she started.

"If you want to put a stop to it, we'll have to. Whoever did this is escalating. Prank phone calls are one thing, but this person is marking on the Bible and using a knife. What's next?"

Then he brought the reality even more clearly to her, "No one should be in this building alone. It's not safe. And, Pastor, the phone tap went to the same six homes as before: Bertha, Minnie, Tess and Grady, Mack, Eva and George, Alberta and Alton."

"It was probably a legitimate phone call," she said. "It couldn't be any of them."

* * *

Shaken, Suzanne went to each elder's home, interrupting their Easter dinners. Alton and Alberta invited her to sit down and eat. She declined food but sat down at the table for a moment. "The phone tap went to the same homes as before so that's no help. Renfro is at the church dusting for fingerprints. He thinks we'd better take this seriously, says the person is becoming more destructive, and we shouldn't be in the building alone. He says we need to get every member fingerprinted so he can compare with what they find on the Bible and the butcher knife."

"Fingerprint our own members?" Alton sputtered.

* * *

Mack and Junior were having dinner with Eva and George so she again sat at a beautifully set table full of the usual dishes: turkey and dressing, mashed potatoes, cranberry relish, sweet potatoes with marshmallows, green bean casserole. Her stomach growled; but she resisted, knowing her family was waiting for her to begin their Easter dinner, cooked the day before and waiting to be warmed up.

She explained that the phone tap went to the same six phones as the other time they had tried to figure this out. Then she tried to keep her voice calm when telling them about the fingerprinting. George, as expected, was furious. His face and head turned from pink to red, and he left the table coughing. Mack and Junior listened quietly. Eva said, "I sure hope we can think of another way to handle this."

Suzanne agreed. "It seems intrusive. It bothers me, but I can't quite put words to it. Somehow it just doesn't seem right. Let's all think it over and meet at the church tomorrow evening with Renfro. I'll see if Dr. Talley can come, too."

* * *

The meeting was short. Renfro was sensitive in the way he presented the information and the need to fingerprint. "The sheriff agrees with me. This has gone on a long, long time; and whoever it is has a lot of anger. We don't know how it might be expressed next."

There was no other way to move forward that they could think of. Dr. Talley had no suggestions except to say, "Seems extreme, but I don't know what else you can you do at this point. Someone is severely troubled and this will certainly smoke her out. But this may also be the time to consider closing the church."

Alton quickly responded to that. "I think all the members will agree to being fingerprinted. Let's ask them to come but not try to force anyone. If somebody doesn't agree, we'll face that later."

Renfro agreed to begin with that and again cautioned them not to be in the building alone. "When we find out who it is, we'll deal with him or her carefully, but this has got to stop," Renfro said.

God, help us. What if it's Minnie, what if it's George, what if it's . . . ?

CHAPTER 46

To Be or Not To Be
Fingerprinted

George stood outside the church on the Sunday after Easter talking to Alton. From inside Suzanne heard him every time the door opened. "This is the stupidest . . . . Why in God's name are you . . . ?"

She started to go out to talk with him, but Eva put her hand on Suzanne's arm. "It's no use. No way is he gonna let himself be fingerprinted, and he's ordered me not to do it either." She set her lips firmly. "I'm sorry but he's trying to convince others not to come, too."

Mack told her George was saying, "They can't treat us like criminals. We done nothing wrong."

"He's telling people that once they were fingerprinted they be put in a file somewhere. And in that file they put everything about you, all your relatives and friends even your bank information. He says you won't believe how much they can know and use against you. That's not true, is it?" Mack asked.

When Suzanne, Alton and Mack went by to talk with George on Monday, he shook his head and walked out the back door leaving them with Eva. They watched him rev the truck and take off up the road leaving a ball of dust behind him.

"He'll calm down," Eva said. "I told him this just makes him look guilty."

Suzanne watched her carefully but couldn't tell if she thought that was a possibility.

"Well, we tried," Alton said. "Even if some people don't show up, we'll narrow the possibilities."

As Suzanne drove the men back to the church, she asked, "Do you think George is capable of doing the damage in the church?"

There was silence. Then Mack said, "He's mean enough to."

CHAPTER 47

Fingerprinting

*D*eputies Renfro and Finn were getting out of their car at the grain elevator as Suzanne pulled in beside them. As usual church members were early and filled all the parking spaces in front of the church. The three entered the door to the basement and when they reached the bottom of the stairs, quiet snaked around the room. "Hello, everybody," Suzanne said in a voice that she hoped carried optimism and not dread. "I'd like you to meet Deputies Renfro and Finn. Maybe some of you know them." She saw Mack elbow Junior and grin. "They are going to help us um . . . do what we've decided to do. We'll wait until everybody gets here before we ask them to give us instructions."

The men gathered around Deputy Renfro. "Hey, Buddy," Mack said, "you play basketball any more? Remember that time we whipped you boys?"

"Renfro, you should've asked me before you took that new job." Alton said. "We don't never need the sheriff out here so we'll have to be dreaming up mischief to give you some work."

While Renfro talked to the men, Finn set up his equipment on the kitchen counter. The women huddled around the gas stove even though it was a perfect May evening, and Suzanne joined them until the chatter began to wind down. It was ten after seven. A quick look at her list showed nearly everyone was there. As expected George and Eva were not, and there were three women from Salina who had said they couldn't come at night. Tess and Grady weren't there either. Bertha whispered, "Tess had a dinner in town. She'll be a little late, and it's not unusual for the cattle to hold Grady up."

Mack overheard her and said in a loud voice, "Old Grady's probably putting his bulls to sleep, singing them lullabies. You think I'm kidding, but I bet he does. He's got him some kinda voice, loved to sing, used to sing in church."

"Voice like an angel," Bertha said. "You could always tell he meant the words he was singing. Even as a boy he was deep in his faith."

"They'll be here soon," Mack said, looking at the clock, "but we could go ahead and start."

Suzanne began with a short prayer. "Lord, we hope we're doing the right thing here. Help us all. Help the one who is anxious and afraid tonight. Help us follow the example of Jesus' kind of love as we move forward."

Several people muttered, "Amen."

Finn explained the process. "One at a time, you'll come over here to the counter and fill out a card with your basic information and sign it. Then I'll put ink on your fingers and I'll help you roll them just so, one at a time. Any questions?"

"Will you tell us what you find out tonight?" Alton asked.

"No, it will take four to six weeks to get the results. When I've got your prints, you can wash the ink off. Then you can go on or stay and visit as far as I'm concerned."

Several people lined up and began the process. Eva came in quietly and stood in line. She didn't mention George. Ten minutes later he came in;

and Suzanne was alert, wondering if he would try to drag Eva home. But he got in line with her and nobody said anything.

It went smoothly, and soon there were only a few people left to fingerprint when Tess rushed in. She was out of breath. "Is Grady here?" she asked.

"No, we haven't seen him," Suzanne told her. "Is he coming?"

"Yes, I was going to meet him here."

"Do you want to call?" Suzanne asked.

"I did. He maybe out walking . . . like he does." Tess looked around and twisted her wedding ring nervously. "Did everybody show up?"

"Almost everybody. Looks like you're the last one, and there are only three people ahead of you now so you might as well go ahead.," Suzanne said.

Tess turned quickly and headed up the back stairs to the sanctuary. "I'll see if he's upstairs."

Suzanne waited a moment then followed her. Tess stood in front of Jesus and the Lambs looking intently at the painting. She swayed like a stalk of wheat in the wind. Suzanne moved closer, ready to catch her if she fainted. Then she saw what Tess was staring at. The lamb in Jesus' arms had a red slit across its throat and blood flowed down onto Jesus' hand. There were even droplets on the floor. Suzanne caught her as she fell backward, sat her down gently and held her head in her lap. She heard someone coming up the stairs. It was Bertha. Suzanne whispered, "Would you ask Deputy Renfro to come up here?" Bertha took one look at Tess, turned quickly and went back downstairs.

Renfro came quickly and stooped down to take Tess's pulse. She opened her eyes at his touch and closed them again. Suzanne nodded to the picture. "It wasn't like that when I left this afternoon."

The sheriff touched the blood on the floor. "Paint," he said.

Tess opened her eyes and jumped to her feet. "We've got to find Grady."

* * *

Suzanne went with Tess and the deputy. Bertha agreed to lock up and give Finn a ride to Tess's when everyone left.

"Keep those fingerprints secure," Renfro told Finn. "We'll see about doing Grady and Tess's when you get to their house."

Renfro drove through the dark countryside. Tess sat in the front seat with her eyes closed.

The sky had cleared after a cloudy and wet day and the stars looked close. The quarter moon cast the only light on the shadowy fields of wheat.

When they pulled in at the farm, Lassie ran up to the car barking. Tess opened the door before they fully stopped. "There's a light in the lean-to." She jumped from the car, and ran behind Lassie. She slid on the wet grass, then kicked her shoes off and ran barefoot. Renfro slipped and fell. Suzanne stepped out of her shoes, and ran after Tess.

She disappeared around the house. When Suzanne reached the lean-to shed at the side of the barn, she saw a light shining down on the tractor and she heard Lassie whining in front of it.

She moved closer. Tess stood stiff and staring. Grady lay curled up, asleep in front of the tractor wrapped in a blanket as though he were camping out. The remains of his dinner lay behind him on a bench, an empty china plate and cup, a thermos. It looked like he had rolled in his sleep almost under the tractor, up against the tire on the driver's side. Lassie lay beside him, head on paws, whimpering.

Before Suzanne knew what was happening, Tess suddenly took two steps toward Grady and kicked Lassie out of the way. Grady looked as peaceful as a child who has been tucked in for the night. Suzanne expected him to wake up.

Renfro caught up to them, held the back of his hand in front of Grady's mouth, and felt on his neck for a pulse. He shook his head.

When he rolled him over, the blanket fell away, and they could see Grady's eyes staring at something beyond them. There was a gun in his hand. Blood soaked his chest and the blanket under him.

Renfro ran out. Suzanne heard him vomiting next to the barn. She turned back toward Tess to offer a shoulder, an arm, a word, whatever she might accept; but Tess had the gun and was aiming it at Lassie. Suzanne knocked her hand; the bullet flew out the back of the shed into the field. Then Renfro was there taking the gun with one hand and wiping his mouth with the other.

"He'd never stop grieving," Tess said in that tiny voice of hers.

Not sure what comfort Tess would accept, Suzanne tentatively put her arm around her shivering shoulders and began moving her away from the scene. She let Suzanne half walk, half carry her to the kitchen door. Static echoed in the still night as Renfro radioed from his car.

The door was unlocked. The kitchen smelled of fish. She took Tess inside to the living room, wrapped a quilt around her on the sofa and after a few minutes left her long enough to make tea. While the water was heating, Suzanne retrieved her shoes and Tess's from the yard.

Bertha and Finn were out at the road talking with Renfro, their voices rising and falling with the wind.

Tess sipped the tea. "He's taken everything," she murmured and then lay down and closed her eyes. Occasionally she took a sharp breath that ended in a sob. Suzanne sat in the recliner next to her, watching intently until there was no movement or sound for a few minutes. Then she leaned the chair back and closed her eyes.

* * *

Cars stopped and started, voices called out in the front and side yards. Nobody disturbed them for a long time. Tess seemed to be sleeping. Suzanne's mind raced and her body began to tremble. *I wonder what I can do to comfort Tess when she wakes up.*

Why would Grady do this? Why now? Suzanne kept trying to push away the image of Grady's eyes and the blood. *He's gone.* Her overloaded mind shut down, and numbness took over.

Renfro came in. Tess opened her eyes and quickly shut them. "We've done what we could tonight," he whispered to Suzanne and motioned her into the kitchen. "I've cordoned off the area over . . . uh, back there and stationed a man at the road where he can see that nobody disturbs anything. His name is Lonnie and he can see your front door. I'm going out this way. Lock the door behind me and be sure the front one is secured, too.

"Pastor, are you okay to stay with her tonight?" She nodded. "Do you want to call someone else to come be with you?" She shook her head.

He handed her a card. "This is the number to call if you need anything. Lonnie will get the word and come right away to the front door. Are you sure you don't want someone else to be here?"

"We're fine." Suzanne said automatically. She didn't want someone there who might feel compelled to talk.

Renfro shook his head and looked at his feet. "I'm awful sorry about this. Grady was a good man. We went to school together. He had too much sadness in his life. Maybe he just couldn't take it any more." He shook his head and wiped away a tear. "Tomorrow, we'll figure out more. Tomorrow."

"It is suicide, isn't it?" she said.

"There's little doubt. It looks like he placed the gun right where he could shoot into his heart and rolled up in that blanket with just enough room to pull the trigger. But the coroner will rule on it. There are some questions that need answering. There's usually a note, but we didn't find one yet.

"We'll look tomorrow. I'll be here first thing. We never did get Grady fingerprints, but we'll get them now and I guess we'll may as well get hers, too."

"Couldn't you just take a glass she has drunk out of instead of upsetting her?"

"You've been watching too much TV," he said. "But, you're right, that will be less difficult for her . . . and for us."

Suzanne called Bell. "Bell, we've had a tragedy out here. It's Grady. Suicide. No, don't come. Take care of the kids. I'm going to stay all night with Tess. I'm okay, but . . . . Well, I'm too tired to even tell you."

CHAPTER 48

After Death

*S*uzanne woke up a few times when Tess moaned. Then when the clock struck three, she heard voices and went to the window. Mack and Lonnie were at the road talking, Lonnie pointing toward the barn. She couldn't hear what they were saying but she could imagine the exchange that would happen many times in the next day or so.

"Who is it?" Tess asked. Suzanne wondered if she'd been asleep at all.

"Mack. Why would he be out in the middle of the night?"

"Woman friend . . . Salina."

Mack had a woman in his life? She couldn't imagine it. One more thing she didn't know about her people.

"You need anything?" she asked Tess.

"He's taken everything."

The rest of the night was quiet. Sleep, no sleep, it didn't matter to Suzanne if she could just stop thinking. *All I need to do right now is provide what comfort I can for Tess. I'll think about what this means later.*

A car door slammed. Voices rose and fell. Morning. A gun shot rang out. Tess wasn't on the couch.

Suzanne slipped her sandals on and ran out the kitchen door. Renfro called to her from a few yards away. "I need you out here," he said with a catch in his voice. She heard Tess crying hysterically. He held a gun in his palm. "She shot his dog, trying to put him out of his misery, I guess."

Suzanne followed him into the barn. Inside in the dusty light, Lonnie held Tess's pencil thin arm awkwardly. Lassie lay on the ground, whining and trying to lick her front left leg. Mack was petting her head and talking to her.

"The bullet grazed her leg," he said. "I'm sorry I didn't see what was happening. Junior and I was down there getting the feed ready. The vet will be here soon. If Grady was here, he'd know how to fix her up."

Tess stared at the ground.

The smell transported Suzanne back to her grandfather's barn: manure, straw, and warm animals. Black bulls looked comfortable in their wooden stalls lining both sides of the long barn. They studiously ignored each other as well as the strangers who disturbed their morning ritual. One wide-eyed, broad and muscular body snorted and turned away to fold his bulk down into the straw.

Suzanne put her arm around Tess and began to move her back to the house. Then she noticed the paintings. They hung above the stalls. Her eyes followed them down one side, across the back and up the other side over the door to the lean-to, and on to where she stood. Painting after painting of animals, their skin transparent in places.

Tess wouldn't move. She was surprisingly strong. Suzanne said, "It would be best for you to go to the house." And they moved on, Tess a zombie under Suzanne's arm.

As she passed the paintings Suzanne saw that they were all realistic. Each one pictured an animal which had met with an accident. She saw a car, a tractor, a scythe.

Tess stopped moving at the stall nearest the barn entrance. Unlike the others it had a door and walls. The door stood open and Tess stared into the room. Paintings hung randomly on the walls to the right and left, and bookshelves covered the back wall. An easel in the corner held a blank canvas and next to it was a table piled with jars and paint tubes.

One of the pictures on the left wall showed a pig impaled on a pitchfork. It looked like the pig had fallen. Its face scrunched up, and Suzanne could almost hear it squealing. By making its body transparent, Grady had shown the tines piercing the stomach and the heart. In the painting next to it, a horse lay on a path, writhing in pain, its transparent leg caught in a trap, a broken bone protruding.

CHAPTER 49

Sarah and Sam

"Sarah, this is Pastor Suzanne from the Harvest church. I'm with your mother. And, Sarah, we've had a terrible tragedy out here." She paused. "It's about your dad. I'm so sorry. He's gone."

"What, what did you say?"

"It's your dad, Sarah."

She gasped. "Oh, no. What's wrong?"

"A gunshot wound. I'm sorry. He didn't make it."

"But, no, not . . . oh, my God. How?"

"We were waiting for him at the church last night. When he didn't come, we brought your mother home and found him. The Deputy is here trying to sort it out. He's talking to your mother in the kitchen right now."

"Oh, my God. Oh, my God."

"Sarah, is there someone I can call to be with you, maybe someone who could drive you here?"

"No, no. I can do it. Did you call Sam yet?"

"No. And, Sarah, think about the driving. It can be dangerous when you've had a big shock like this."

"Okay, I'll call Sam and talk it over. We should be able to get there by mid to late afternoon." She choked back a sob.

Suzanne sighed a long breath, releasing tension, and leaned back in the chair where she had spent the night. Over the years, she had thought long and hard about the best way to deliver bad news. She decided it was best to alert the person that something is wrong, pause to let them prepare themselves, then reveal the loss, giving details only as they ask for them.

But she wasn't sure anything she did could lessen the shock or the grief. She had walked that road with many parishioners, and each one handled it differently.

The voices from the kitchen were a low drone with an occasional louder whine. Suzanne welcomed the break from Tess. She closed her eyes and took a deep breath. Sarah was a hospice nurse. That might help her deal with this. But what would this do to Tess? She'd had too much loss for one lifetime. People worried about Grady because he had been driving the tractor when his son died. *But Tess had to have been devastated. Her little boy, only five years old. And now Grady is gone, too.*

* * *

Members of the church and people from the community came in a steady stream, all carrying food. Tess sat at the kitchen table like a stone while women held her hand and men patted her on the back. Bertha welcomed people and filled the silence, thanking each one on Tess's behalf. Eva and Alberta hovered, managing the kitchen and offering food to family and friends.

Bell arrived. "Suze, you need to go home and get some sleep."

"I know, I know, but I've got to wait and see Tess and Grady's children. This is going to be difficult for them."

She moved from kitchen to living room to porch visiting with those who came while Bell sat in the living room talking with Tess's brother Leonard and his wife Saralou who were members of his church.

The clergy group - every one of them - came and stood out in front of the house with Suzanne. She felt encircled with their love and support even though their words didn't penetrate her mind.

Danny Canny came. *Ambulance chaser*, Suzanne thought, then chastised herself and tried to remember the day he had shown her the photo album when she spotted the lonely little boy in him. He joined Renfro on the front porch.

Suzanne moved in a daze trying to think what she should do as their pastor.

When Sarah and Sam drove up, she met them outside. "Your mother may seem unaware of what has happened. She's probably still in shock," she told them.

"How did he die?" Sam asked.

Suzanne cleared her throat but her voice came out hoarse and wavering. "It looks like a self-inflicted gunshot wound."

At the look of horror on Sarah's face, she put her arm around her shoulders. "Deputy Renfro is here somewhere and he'll tell you more."

They went around the house to the kitchen. Alberta held the door open, greeted them and then left. Bertha and Eva were fussing with the food, and Tess sat at the table. She moved her stare from the food to her children but said nothing.

Bertha hugged the two children. "I'm so sorry, dear. I'm so sorry."

"Sam, Sarah, this is a terrible tragedy," Eva said.

Tess sat silent and stiff. Sarah and Sam hugged her, but it was awkward. She didn't move.

"We're here now," Sarah said.

"We're here now, Mother. We'll take care of things," Sam assured her.

Renfro came in from the barn. "You probably don't remember me," he said. "I went to school with your dad. Haven't seen you for years. I'm sorry for your loss."

To their questions, he simply said, "We don't know exactly what happened, but we're working on it."

They wanted to go outside, to see, to know. Renfro started out the door with them and turned back to Suzanne, squinting his eyes at her, a silent plea to come help. She followed and replayed the night before as they walked to the barn. "We were at church in the basement, he didn't come. When your mother got there we found the painting in the sanctuary damaged, drove here with her and found him there in front of the tractor." Suzanne breathed a sigh of relief. Someone had placed a blanket over the spot where he had lain and there was no blood showing.

Renfro said, "The coroner will make a ruling. We have to investigate, you understand."

Sam stared at the blanket in front of his feet. Sarah's eyes filled and overflowed.

There was nothing more to do there. They went back to the kitchen.

Suzanne's arms felt heavy, her feet were difficult to pick up and put down again, and her eyes wouldn't focus. She agreed to leave her car at the church and let Bell take her home.

* * *

Her bed felt cool and soft. She slept twelve hours, waking in time to see the children off to school.

"Did he kill himself? Was he the one who did stuff in the church?" Peter asked.

"And the phone calls and notes?" Julie said. "Did he kill himself because of the fingerprinting? Maybe he knew everybody would find out and he didn't want to——."

Suzanne wanted to know, too.

"I don't know. I don't know," Suzanne said. "But when I find out I will tell you the truth. It's terrible, terrible; but we'll surround the family with our love. With God's help we'll get through this together."

After they left, Bell lingered. "What can I do? What do you need?"

"You don't need to stay," she said. "I'm okay." But even as she said that, the tears plopped out of her eyes, and ran down her cheeks. Bell held her hand and let her cry.

"What have I done?" she asked. "What have I done?"

"Oh, Suze, you haven't caused this. Surely, you're not going to blame yourself."

"You told me not to stay out there. Alton told me I didn't understand the people. George said leave it alone, Dr. Talley said don't get involved. I should have listened, should have listened," she sobbed. "I didn't know what to do."

CHAPTER 50

Questions

*W*hen Suzanne returned to see Tess the next morning, she was in her room asleep. Half a dozen women sat in the kitchen talking, and Sam and Sarah were in the living room. "Pastor," Sam said, "would you go with Sarah and me to the church? I want to see if I can fix the picture before Sunday morning."

At the church he examined the red paint on the lamb's throat while Sarah and Suzanne sat in the choir chairs and watched. Sam's blond hair fell over his face as he studied the lamb with boyish intensity.

Peter will look like him in a few years, Suzanne thought. *And Julie will be Sarah's age before I know it.* Tears kept dripping down Sarah's face, a beautiful face. Her skin was smooth and flawless, ivory with rosy round cheeks.

"It's hard to believe Dad would take his own life," Sarah said. "Deputy Renfro says maybe he took some pills to help him get up the courage. They found an empty sleeping pill jar in the kitchen."

"Dad never would take pills," Sam said. "He always told us to eat well and not depend on vitamins. He wouldn't even take an aspirin when he had one of his bad headaches."

"Yes, years ago Mother tried to get him to take one of her sleeping pills." Sarah said. "Remember? It was when she complained that he kept her awake with his nightmares."

"I remember hearing him crying at night," Sam added.

"Why do you think that was?" Suzanne asked.

"Billy," Sam said.

"Everything was about that," Sarah said.

Sam squeezed out paint on the piece of cardboard he was using for a palette. "We were both born after Billy died; but he was always in the house, a ghost of sadness and anger hovering in the middle of every room."

"Did you notice Dad acting any different lately? Any idea why now?" Sarah asked.

"I don't know." Suzanne told her what she did know including the phone calls, the notes, the Easter damage and resulting fingerprinting decision. "The fingerprinting may have left no way out for him. I would never have okayed that if I could have thought of another way."

"Oh, don't think that it's your fault," Sarah said. "We don't think so." She looked at Sam who nodded.

"None of it makes sense, he said. "Dad would never have damaged this painting. And he wouldn't have treated the Bible and communion table like that."

"He found great comfort in this church," Sarah said. "Sometimes he'd just come and sit here looking at Jesus holding the little lamb. He told me once that sometimes that lamb was Billy, sometimes himself, other times Sam or me. . . ." She sobbed uncontrollably. Suzanne handed her a tissue and put an arm around her shoulder. They sat there quietly while Sam finished painting over the red marks on the lamb's throat and the drips that looked like blood.

"You've obviously painted with oils before," Suzanne said noticing the detailed shading into the original colors. "When it dries, I don't think you'll be able to tell." He looked pleased.

"What do you think the paintings in the barn meant for your dad?" she asked.

Sarah took a deep shuddering breath and wiped her eyes, "I don't know. Mom always said it was his crazy coming out."

"I think it had to do with Billy's death and the way he died," Sam said. "Somehow it seems to be tied up with that."

"Could it be his way of grieving about Billy," Suzanne asked, "a way to keep feeling the pain or maybe a way to express it?"

They were quiet. "I'm sorry," Suzanne said. "I don't know. I have no way of knowing."

"No . . . no, it's okay," Sam said. "I never thought about it that way. But it could be. It's clear he was working something out."

Sarah nodded. "His grief. And I've always thought it was Mom's grief that made her angry with everyone, especially with Dad. I don't remember her ever being happy."

"She resented any peace Dad found," Sam said.

* * *

They went back to the house to plan the funeral service. Bertha was there and Danny Canny had arrived. "The coroner will release Grady's body on Monday so we'll have the service on Tuesday morning," he said.

"Is that what you want, Tess, Sarah, Sam?"
Suzanne asked. *I will not let him make this decision for the family and me. He should do what they want and ask if I'm available, not just assume.*

"I'd prefer Wednesday morning if it's possible for everyone," Sam said. "Are you available, Pastor?"

Aha, he's pretty sharp. "Yes, I can do that."

When Danny and Bertha left, Suzanne sat with Tess and her children in the living room and talked about the service. Sarah and Sam told stories about their dad, how he walked all over the county even at night, how he loved his bulls and painting pictures. They told his account of finding the first Lassie the day his brother died. They had many good memories.

Sarah sat on the floor petting Lassie whose leg was still bandaged. The vet had said she would heal fine, and Sarah had claimed her for her own.

Suzanne asked Tess, "How did you and Grady meet?" But Tess stared out the window and didn't answer.

The children prodded her, but she wouldn't talk except to say, "It's not important now."

* * *

Suzanne stayed strong as long as she was with them. But when she got home, she collapsed, weepy and tired. She woke up to eat a slice of pizza Bell brought to her in bed.

"Bertha called," he said. "The coroner has ruled it a suicide" he said. "She wants to know if you'd like her to get the word around so you don't have to announce it Sunday."

Suzanne nodded. *Sunday. Worship. Sermon.*

CHAPTER 51

The Sunday After
May 1987

Suzanne stepped into the pulpit and gripped it hard, but it failed to steady her. She scanned the small congregation, her eyes resting on one face and then another, ending with the tearful faces of her children in the back pew. During the Call to Worship and first hymn, the people leaned toward her as if she were a powerful magnet.

She had seen the storm approaching earlier when she and the children left Salina. As they drove out to the country church, they saw gray clouds far out west rolling over the Kansas plains. By the time she pulled up in front of the church, the storm was closer and darker. Purplish black clouds boiled and raged rushing toward the little church which sat in the midst of miles and miles of fields.

The room grew dark pulling the small group closer to each other; and the candles on the communion table gave off an uncertain light, their flames fluttering in the disturbed air. "Let us confess our sins," she said.

Soon after she began the worship service, the storm was overhead. The rain built steadily from a drumbeat to a fury and before long the pounding on the roof drowned out the songs and responses. But the people followed along as always, bowing their heads for prayer and singing the familiar words:

> As it was in the beginning,
> is now and ever shall be,
> World without end. Amen. Amen.

Suzanne glanced down, but the fluorescent light glowed harshly on the empty pulpit. No order of worship and no manuscript prompted her today. "We've journeyed far over the past few months," she said, "and we've persevered through all the anguish and confusion. This week's tragedy has brought us some answers, but it has also brought grief and . . . and regret." Lightning flashed and froze the moment. Seconds later thunder shook the room.

She raised her voice to be heard. "I keep asking myself what I could have done to prevent this dreadful death." She tried to wipe away the tears with one swipe, but they kept coming. She stopped to dry her eyes and regain her composure.

Their stricken eyes and hers connected. "My God, what have we done?" she said over the roaring wind and rain. She lowered her fist. "What have we done?"

They were all there, even Minnie's sons from California who came in with a huge spray of flowers and sat with their mother, all three unusually subdued. Tess sat in her pew with Sarah and Sam. Bertha's daughter Ellen played the piano, and Ellen's daughter Mary rang the bell with Peter's help.

When Julie and Peter sang "The Lord Is My Shepherd, I'll Not Want," Suzanne heard many sniffles. *We need the faith of children today,* she thought as she watched them singing in front of Jesus the Great Shepherd.

Her first impulse had been to leave them at home, to shield them from so much sadness; but Peter said, "Aren't we part of the church?" Julie had nodded. Suzanne had no answer to that. Of course, they were part of the congregation. And their music was healing.

Suzanne read the scripture lesson from Hebrews which kept repeating "by faith," by faith Abel, by faith Enoch, Noah, Abraham, Sarah and so on. "Each one persevered through difficult times by faith," she said. "They all managed through the worst of days, by their faith." Suzanne raised her voice to be heard. "Let me hear from you this morning. What are you thinking and how is your faith is sustaining you?"

After a pause, Mack spoke up. "Grady was a good man. He had a hard life. I always was afraid he'd do something like this. If only we hadn't pushed for knowing everything, well, maybe he wouldn't have—you know. I keep wondering what we could have done to make this turn out different."

There were murmurs of agreement. Suzanne glanced at Tess. She was staring straight ahead at the pew in front of her.

She saw Alberta nudge Alton with her elbow. He lifted his chin from the top of his cane and said, "I was against that business of fingerprinting, at first. But there seemed no other way to go. Then, after this, I wondered if we done the right thing . . . seeing as how it turned out."

Suzanne held her breath.

"But after thinking it through, Alberta and I agree we had no choice. If we hadn't done something, we'd have had to close the church. It was getting to be too much, especially Easter."

Bertha spoke up. "You know, we did the best we could. And we were loving toward each other as we went along."

"Mostly," Minnie said looking over at George who looked down at his knees.

"We searched for the truth. That's never wrong," Eva said.

"We've talked about evil, but I can't think that anyone in this church is evil," Bertha added.

Peter spoke up. "That's what I wanted to say."

Bertha nodded to Peter and went on, "Remember last year when that Challenger Space Shuttle exploded and we all gathered here? Pastor Bill preached about bad things happening to good people."

She paused letting the thunder take over then went on. "I'm thinking maybe all we can do is make good choices and leave the rest to God. Like this weather. If it turns into hail, we could lose our wheat. If it doesn't, we're looking at a mighty good harvest. But whatever happens we'll go on."

Minnie clapped and the rest joined in.

Later that day Suzanne reviewed the morning. *It sounds like nobody blames me, but if I had listened to Alton and hadn't kept trying to solve the problem; if I had worked harder to break through the walls around Grady . . . .*

* * *

On Wednesday they celebrated Grady's life. The church was full, even the basement. Speakers appeared out of nowhere, set up downstairs so people could hear the service.

Tears flowed freely. There were no answers.

"He came from a place we don't know, God, and now we offer him back into your arms. We commit his body to your loving care, his soul to your mercy."

CHAPTER 52

The Last Picture

Sam has found something in Grady's barn," Bertha said when Suzanne answered the phone. "Can you come see what you think?"

"A note?" Suzanne asked turning off the typewriter and grabbing her keys.

"It may be as good as one."

When she arrived, Bertha and Sam stood in the barn amid packing boxes full of Grady's paintings. Sarah ran in shortly after Suzanne. "Mother's asleep," she said.

"Look," Sam said pointing to the easel. "I found it in his sketch book." An arrow pierced the heart of Jesus and the hearts of others standing in front of him and behind him. The figures were overlapped and one long arrow curved to penetrate each one at precisely the spot of Grady's fatal wound. Blood dripped from their hearts as they stood in a long arc. Jesus was realistic and recognizable, shown with the expected beard, hair, and gentle eyes. He looked straight ahead, his arms spread wide as though he were on the cross. Behind him each shadowy figure's arms were a little higher until the last figure's arms were reaching overhead, fingers nearly touching, eyes following their hands. They looked like a sequence of ballet poses. In front of Jesus their arms were lower and lower until the first one's arms were curved downward, eyes on an outline of a cradled lamb.

"See," Sam said, "It's his suicide note. The last one is Dad. If you look close, you can see a scar over his right eye. It's from that time he got hit with a rock."

Suzanne stared and then rubbed her eyes.

Bertha wiped away tears. "He didn't lose his faith. I was afraid the paint on the church picture meant that he thought God had taken his little Billy as a sacrifice. But this lamb isn't being sacrificed. It's held and protected."

Suzanne nodded. "Jesus and the others are hurt – with the arrow through each one's heart."

"Yes!" Bertha said. "I think that's it. They're all making a sacrifice like Jesus did. Like in your sermon, it's the ultimate response to evil. 'Greater love has no man than this, that he lay down his life for his friends.' That's what would fit with the Grady I know."

Oh, no, Suzanne thought, *because of my sermon?*

Sarah said, "Bertha, if this shows a sacrifice— if he was laying down his life out of love for his friends, who do you think it was for?"

Bertha held her hands to her lips in praying position. "Could be for the church . . . could be for your mother." She shook her head. "I don't know. It doesn't come together as well as I first thought."

Sam stood with one finger touching the picture, making no attempt to brush away the tears dripping from his chin. "Anytime I saw Dad painting, he was crying."

Sarah stood with hands on hips. "Well, why would he paint the lamb in the church as though its neck were cut?" she asked. "Why would he send nasty notes and make phone calls? None of this makes sense to me."

CHAPTER 53

Harvest

*I*n the six weeks between Easter and Pentecost, life drifted into late spring. One day Suzanne stopped the car next to a field she passed every day and rolled down the window. All the way to the horizon, "amber waves of grain" rolled and danced in the wind. The wheat had changed during the spring months. A luscious, dark emerald green lightened when the seeds developed. Then light green turned to yellow green; and then miles of uninterrupted fields shone like sunshine, a yellow gold which then matured into burnished gold ready for harvesting.

A few fields had already been taken in, and people were starting to relax. There was no forecast of rain, no threat of hail.

At first there was much talk about why Grady would cause chaos in the church. Mack got angry after church one Sunday when George said, "The man just couldn't take it. Too much guilt. He must of flipped out."

"You'll never convince me," Mack said. "He might of took his life, but he would not have written 'Lies' on the Bible or done some of that other stuff."

Mack interrupted George another time when he was describing the "crazy pictures in the barn."

He informed everybody within hearing what he thought about that. "You don't understand Grady at all. I think he wanted to be a vet, and that was his way of studying animals and trying to help them."

The talk settled down after a while but Suzanne knew that unanswered questions lay under the surface of their lives. Renfro had said fingerprint results would be back in four to six weeks, and now it had been six weeks so she was trying to prepare herself for the uproar to come. *What if Mack's right? What will happen if Grady's fingerprints aren't found on the knife and Bible?*.

Phone calls had been normal since Grady's death. But one day Suzanne answered the phone at church and no one was there.

It's an accident, she told herself.

It rang a second time. No one was there. Her chest felt heavy and her hands trembled. *Please, God, not again.*

A third time it rang.

"Tess?" she asked.

Her hunch was rewarded. A timid voice answered. "Yes."

"How are you today?"

"Fine"

"Would this be a good time for me to come see you?"

"Okay," Tess said.

Then Sarah was on the other end.

"Sarah, is this a good time for me to visit?"

"Sure, come on over."

"Tell me, is there a phone in the barn?"

"No, why?"

"I'll tell you when I get there."

At first Suzanne had seen Tess twice a week while she was still in shock trying to come to terms with Grady's death. Tess talked little and seemed diminished, smaller and less of a force to be reckoned with. However, Suzanne continued visiting her, usually sitting quietly, drinking tea and praying silently while Tess concentrated on her embroidery. But now she had missed a couple of weeks. It was time to go.

* * *

While Sarah fixed tea, Suzanne sat in the recliner she had slept in that terrible night. Tess was on the couch, embroidering as usual.. Suzanne sat in a comfortable silence watching her fingers. *There may come a time when she wants to talk about it. I should keep visiting at least once a week.*

Lassie lay near Tess as she usually did, head on paws, watching her with what looked to Suzanne like great love. Unreasonable, unconditional love.

Suzanne watched those hands putting in tiny stitches, but after a few moments realized she was staring. When her eyes focused, Suzanne found herself looking at Tess's shoes. They were the same shoes she had worn the night Grady died, the ones she had kicked off in the wet grass. Memories flooded in bringing tears to her eyes.

When Sarah came in with tea, Suzanne was wiping her eyes. "Is anything wrong?" she asked.

"Oh, it's little things that grab me sometimes. I noticed that your mother is wearing the sandals she wore the night your dad died. We both kicked our shoes off in the wet grass when we were running to the barn. Seeing them brought that night back."

"Oh, yes, I know how that is, but she had been at a DAR meeting, hadn't she?"

"Yes."

Sarah stared at her mother. "You didn't wear sandals to DAR, did you?"

Tess kept putting in stitches as though she hadn't heard her. Then she kicked at Lassie.

"Mother!" Sarah said. "Why do you treat Lassie like that? She adores you. Look at her. Even when you are mean to her she stays right with you. Here, drink this tea and here's a cookie. Eat something, Mother, or at least try to drink some tea." She turned to Suzanne. "She hasn't been eating. It's been several days so I've scheduled an appointment with the doctor for tomorrow."

Suzanne drank her tea, but Tess didn't touch hers or her cookie.

Sarah left to make a quick trip to the post office. "Come on, Lassie, let's go for a ride."

Suzanne tried talking to Tess. "I've been wondering about everything that happened," she said. "We're going to get the fingerprinting results soon. Are you prepared if Grady's prints aren't on the knife and Bible?"

Tess glanced up but said nothing.

"I don't think he was the one causing the disturbances. For one thing he couldn't have been calling you in the middle of the night. At first I thought there might be a phone in the barn, but there isn't, is there? I remember he looked shocked when I mentioned nighttime calls. Didn't you tell me you were getting calls at night?" Tess shook her head and went back to putting stitches in her embroidery.

"Tell me the truth. Did you get phone calls?"

Suzanne saw a slight smile around her lips before they pressed into a firm line again.

"Did you call me one time and say, 'Help me?'"

Tess stopped sewing and looked down at her hands.

"Did you write the notes? Tell me the truth."

Suzanne tapped her on the knee and she looked up. Looking Tess straight in the eyes, she said,

"Was it all you? The communion cloth, the banner? Oh, Tess," she cried, "the red paint on the picture and the Bible?"

She smirked then sneered. Her eyes squinted. Suzanne's stomach froze and chills radiated down her legs and up through her arms and torso.

"No, oh, no, Tess, surely you didn't—."

"He took everything."

"Grady?"

She shook her head.

"Who, who took everything?"

Inside the house there was absolute silence and outside the incessant wind against the shutters.

"God?" Suzanne asked.

Tess looked her in the eye, her teeth clenched and her lips pursed. She nodded.

"I don't understand. Help me understand. God took everything? He took Grady?"

She nodded, "A long time ago."

"You mean when Billy died?"

Suzanne thought she was going to speak then, but she simply looked sad and leaned her head to one side.

"Did you paint red on the lamb's throat?"

Tess stared at her.

"You did, didn't you? Grady wouldn't have. But why? Why did you do that?"

"It's lies, all lies."

Suzanne didn't want to hear this. She wanted to leave but she was frozen. She held onto the arms of her chair.

"That lamb was sacrificed. He killed that lamb," Tess said.

"Jesus?"

"Yes, Jesus." She spat it out. Her eyes squinted and glared at Suzanne.

"Oh, my God, Tess, don't you see that Jesus is protecting that lamb?"

Suzanne stood up.

"You can't see it. You can't see the truth." She spit out her words and some spittle landed on Suzanne's hand. She used every bit of self control not to wipe it off in order to keep eye contact with Tess.

"The lambs are sacrificed. That picture is a lie. It's all lies. You good Christians." She sneered. Her face twisted on itself as though she had eaten something bitter. "You won't look at the truth."

"Oh, my God, Tess. Don't you see what you have done?" Suzanne put her hands on Tess's shoulders wanting to shake her. "Tell me the truth. The fingerprint results will come soon. You'll have to answer to God and the law. Confess now. Ask for forgiveness."

Tess looked up, her mouth open, her face a mask of anger and disgust. Then she wiggled away and reached for her sewing basket.

Too late, Suzanne realized she had cornered a mad woman. A picture flashed in her mind, Tess holding a gun, shooting at Lassie.

She backed toward the kitchen as Tess rose digging in her sewing basket. "Wait, don't tell anybody. Wait, look here."

Suzanne heard a car door slam. Sarah came in the kitchen door before Suzanne could get there. "Renfro was at the post office. He's coming with news—."

"Watch out," Suzanne yelled. "Get back. I think she has a gun."

Sarah stood in the doorway, stunned, "Mother?"

Tess came from the living room into the kitchen, fumbling in her basket. Lassie ran up to her, and she backed away from him, dropping everything. A tiny gun fell on the floor.

Then Renfro was there, grabbing the gun and the sewing basket while Sarah hugged her mother tight and moved her backwards. "Mother. How could you? How could you?" She was crying and yelling, but Tess was silent. "Move," Sarah said. "Move. You have no idea how much trouble you are in."

Renfro and Suzanne looked at each other and simultaneously shook their heads. "Her fingerprints were all over the Bible," he said, "and on the marker she used. They were on the, well, on everything that was done on Easter. It had to have been her doing."

"Do you think she— ?" Suzanne couldn't say it.

"Let's go find out," he said.

* * *

They stood in front of the family photos, Sarah gripping her mother's arms. "Mother, did you do those things?"

"He took away everything."

"She means God," Suzanne said.

"Did you put paint on the lamb?"

Tess spoke through those clenched teeth. "Lambs were sacrificed. That picture was a lie."

"Oh, my God, Mother, what have you done? No, tell me you didn't. Oh, God, please tell me you didn't kill Dad."

Tess held out her hand for her sewing basket, but Renfro kept it away from her.

"No, no, I didn't do that," Tess screeched reaching for it. "I can prove it. Let me show you."

Sarah took the basket from Renfro and keeping it out of reach, pulled out yarn and threads, knitting needles, embroidery hooks and threw them on the floor. And then she found another gun at the bottom of it all, a small handgun. "Mother, for God's sake, where do you get these?"

She handed it to Renfro who unloaded it.

"Here's something else," Sarah said. She held a large manila envelope and pulled out three business envelopes.

Tess reached for it.

"No, Mother. One's addressed to me." She read it and handed it to Suzanne.

> *Sarah, my girl,*
> *I am so sorry to leave you with all this.*
> *I had no idea what was going on.*
> *Maybe some peace will come now.*
> *Take care of your Mother as best you can.*
> *But live your own life.*
>
> *I love you, Dad*

She bent her head to her knees and sobbed. Tess turned and looked out the window.

Renfro picked up the other two envelopes. One addressed to Sam hadn't been opened, but the one to Tess had been. He held it so Suzanne could see it, too.

> *Tess, my dear. I had no idea.*
> *This is all my fault.*
> *I am sorry. I am so sorry.*
> *Please forgive me for everything.*
> *I have always loved you,*
> *and I hope this will free you.*
> *There is a Balm in Gilead.*
>
> *All my love, Grady*

Later, Sarah called Sam and read his letter to him through her tears.

> *Dear Sam,*
> *Please forgive me for doing this*
> *I can't see any other way to make things*

right for your mother.
Take care of her and your sister as best you
are able, but live your own life.
Please take down my pictures.
They always disturbed your mother.
My anatomy professor Dr. White may have
some use for them.

I love you,
Dad

CHAPTER 54

Seedtime and Harvest

Sunday mornings the empty pew, third on the left, reminded the worshipers of their loss. Nobody sat in Grady's seat. He joined all those who had gone on: Bertha's husband, Minnie's husband, George's mother and father and all the others whose lives had been part of this church family, for better or for worse.

Tess's seat remained empty, too. She refused to come to church, but Sarah and Junior now sat together at the end of the pew. Suzanne wasn't surprised when they announced their engagement. Mack and Junior had been running the farm since Grady's death, and she had heard that Junior was eating dinner there most nights.

Sam was home one Sunday and stood up with Sarah at the announcement time. He said, "You have all been kind and generous to us. I know you've been hearing rumors. Sarah and I want to tell you the truth." He paused and cleared his throat. "Dad didn't do the damage to the church or send notes or make phone calls."

There was a collective gasp.

"We don't want you to go on thinking about him that way," Sarah said. "We don't know exactly why all this happened; but Mother——." She blinked back tears. "Mother's grief——." She couldn't go on.

Sam took over. "We don't understand it, and Mother's not explaining. We think maybe her grief got all twisted in her. Now, she's very ill. She has pancreatic cancer and the doctor says she only has months to live. Dad left us notes so we know that he did—." His voice cracked. "We know that he did take his own life. I hope he rests in peace. We hope it's enough that we all know the truth and can stop wondering and talking about it all."

Suzanne expected some anger toward Tess, but if people felt it, they didn't show it at church. The drama slipped under the surface of their lives. Several women in the church and community volunteered to stay with Tess occasionally so Sarah could get out of the house.

Without Tess, there was no pianist until Bertha's daughter Ellen agreed to take turns with Tess's sister-in-law Saralou. She and Leonard moved their membership to Harvest. Then Ellen's daughter Mary, who had been baptized on Easter, began ringing the bell every week with Peter and Julie. And she brought a friend with her. Soon after that Eva started a Sunday School class for the children. And so life went on.

* * *

One day Dr. Talley called Suzanne. "The United Methodists propose that Harvest yoke with their Gypsum church and share a pastor. It's a great opportunity," he told her. "Harvest would only have to pay the pastor one-fourth; the larger church would pick up three-fourths. Our committee thinks it would be good for Harvest. Ask your elders and congregation. If they're in agreement, we'll present a recommendation at the next Presbytery meeting.

There's pressure on us to decide quickly since the Methodists have someone in mind.

"If we do this, you will have about four weeks to wrap up your ministry with them. Also," he added, "I've got a new interim possibility for you. There's a church in a mess. They've run off three pastors in a row and will probably have to close; but after what you've done out there at Harvest, the Committee on Ministry would like you to go in and give it one last shot."

* * *

She talked it over with the clergy group. They laughed at how excited she was about the challenge of the troubled church. "I'm surprised myself," she told them. "I don't know what I'm getting into, but I'll go in and love them and see where that leads."

* * *

On her last Sunday the congregation held a covered dish dinner to say goodbye to Suzanne and her family. Bell even took the Sunday off to be with them. All the members were there and also many others from the community.

Danny Canny and Deputy Renfro came in all smiles telling her that they were going into business together running the Cosby-Canny Funeral Home. Renfro said he was relieved not to have the responsibility of a Deputy. "I'm just not cut out for that kind of work."

Minnie, wearing a large red hat with a sweeping gray feather, interrupted them to give

Suzanne a framed picture of her young and beautiful self. "It's a Hollywood shot from the ooold days," she said.

Alberta presented Suzanne with two gifts from the congregation: a quilt in the beautiful rusts, browns, and golds of harvest and also a framed photograph of all of them sitting in front of Grady's big picture.

They had posed in the choir chairs, waving. Sarah and Junior were in the back row with Minnie and her hat between them. Alberta sat by Alton who was in the center front, chin on cane, smiling with one finger raised in a wave. George held up two fingers behind Alton's head. Eva was caught rolling her eyes at her husband. Bertha stood to one side, her daughter and granddaughter in front of her.

"We're waving goodbye or maybe we're waving hello," Bertha said. Later, she whispered, "You know you're family and I expect you to keep in touch."

"Friends for life," Suzanne said giving her a big hug.

Bell drove them home. All was quiet except for Peter's whispery whistle and drum beat in the back seat. Beside him Julie was studying the picture of the congregation. Suzanne hugged the quilt to her chest looking out the window at the big sky and familiar fields meeting at the horizon.

See the author's website for discussion questions.
www.judymitchellrich.com.

CPSIA information can be obtained at www.ICGtesting.com
Printed in the USA
BVOW021114080413

317582BV00011BA/203/P